"Stop trying to figure me out, Kim."

"I'm not. I just don't believe you'd turn your back on your parents in their time of need."

"Take it from me, Kim. Not everyone wants to be saved. I'm comfortable in my skin, and I am what I am. I don't need a crusader."

"But you'd be so much happier if you—"

"Let it go," Wyatt interrupted forcefully as he started down the landing to the elevator. "You have no idea what's better for me. No idea at all."

"I know Chase is your son." She clamped her hand over her mouth as the words slipped out.

TERRY FOWLER is a native Tar Heel who loves calling coastal North Carolina home. Single, she works full time and is active in her small church. Her greatest pleasure comes in the way God has used her writing to share His message. Her hobbies include gardening, crafts, and genealogical research. Terry invites everyone to visit her Web page at terryfowler.net.

Books by Terry Fowler

HEARTSONG PRESENTS

HP298—A Sense of Belonging
HP346—Double Take
HP470—Carolina Pride
HP537—Close Enough to Perfect
HP629—Look to the Heart
HP722—Christmas Mommy

Except for Grace

Terry Fowler

Heartsong Presents

To all God's disciples who helped me find my way.
 And to Jesus Christ for loving me enough to die for my sins.

A note from the Author:
I love to hear from my readers! You may correspond with me by writing:

Terry Fowler
Author Relations
PO Box 721
Uhrichsville, OH 44683

ISBN 978-1-59789-538-5

EXCEPT FOR GRACE

All scripture quotations are taken from the King James Version of the Bible.

All of the characters and events in this book are fictitious. Any resemblance to actual persons, living or dead, or to actual events is purely coincidental.

Our mission is to publish and distribute inspirational products offering exceptional value and biblical encouragement to the masses.

PRINTED IN THE U.S.A.

one

"You want me to build what?"

"A cross," Kimberly Elliott repeated, focusing on the way his voice had risen with his question. "An old, rugged cross for my Easter program."

Wyatt Alexander ran his hand along the cabinet front he'd been sanding when she let herself into his workroom. "I don't do stuff like that. I build furniture and cabinets."

Kim refused to take no for an answer. This program was too important to her and to Cornerstone Community Church. "Beth says you're the best carpenter she knows."

That got his attention.

"She has to say that. She's my sister."

Kim didn't feel that was the case with Beth. When she had asked her about a carpenter, Beth immediately recommended her brother and proceeded to point out his pieces in her home. Kim recognized Wyatt Alexander's work as quality. "Not every sister holds her brother in such high regard."

He removed his safety glasses, appearing uneasy with the discussion. "Beth's a good sister."

Never having had a sibling, Kim wasn't certain whether his discomfort had more to do with her request or having to say something nice about his kid sister.

She changed tactics and flashed him her most beguiling smile. "I know it's early to be thinking about Easter; but there's so much to do, and I wanted to get this out of the way first thing."

Kim found Wyatt difficult to read. He continued to run his hand over the furniture, frowning slightly before he reached for sandpaper and smoothed it over the piece.

"You have measurements?"

Kim tried not to show her excitement. "It's for a boy about this tall," she explained eagerly, holding her hand about chest high.

She heard his quick intake of breath as he asked, "A boy?"

She nodded. "He'll need a foot stand and pegs to hold on to when he stretches out his arms. The end result should probably be somewhere between six and seven feet tall."

"You have a boy playing Jesus?" Wyatt asked again, sounding incredulous.

"It's a children's play," Kim explained.

"At Cornerstone?" He sounded doubtful.

"How did you know?"

"You're my sister's friend, and since she attends Cornerstone I figured you must, too. So how did you convince them to let you break tradition?"

She knew from his question that Wyatt was more than a little familiar with the church. She didn't recall seeing him there, though. "I asked."

He nodded, a half smile touching his mouth. "Yeah, I can see where you might have worn them down."

His mockery might have offended Kim if she didn't want his help so badly. Then again he wasn't the first to recognize her persistent nature.

Wyatt continued, "I suppose I could turn a couple of landscape timbers into a cross. There's probably enough scrap lumber around here to build a foot rest."

"What are landscape timbers?"

"Those long wooden poles people put around their flower beds. Don't tell me you've never seen them."

She shrugged. "I live in a condo at the beach. The ocean is my yard."

Wyatt sighed heavily. "If you ask at the hardware store, they'll help you find them. Buy two eight-footers and bring them over. I'll work your cross into my schedule."

Kim could have hugged him. Producing this play was one of the most important things in the world to her. "Thanks for your help. I'll be sure to put your name on the program."

"I'd just as soon you didn't." When Kim looked at him, he said, "I don't want people thinking they can ask me to build anything under the sun. You're the exception."

She wondered why but dared not ask. "God appreciates your help."

His grim look expressed his true feelings. "I doubt God cares one way or the other. I'm only agreeing because you're my sister's friend and I owe her."

His feeling that God didn't care stabbed Kim in the heart. She knew how much God loved every one of His children. If only she could make him understand. The feeling she shouldn't antagonize him further was strong. "How much will this cost us?"

"Since I have no idea what the going cost for cross construction is, let's just say this one's on me. You provide the material. I'll provide the manpower."

Kim found his prickly personality difficult to interpret. Not sure if he was joking or not, she decided to play it light. "I think we can afford that. Thanks again. I'll let you get back to work."

He didn't bother to respond when she called good-bye. She exited the crowded and dusty vacant front office, admiring the antique wooden door as she turned the old brass knob. Outside in the parking area the hound that had greeted her earlier with his ominous bark all but shoved his head beneath her hand. Kim caressed his floppy ears and spoke softly to the animal, glancing back at the metal building that housed Alexander Woodworking.

Her gaze stopped on the carved wooden sign that read MEETINGS BY APPOINTMENT OR CHANCE. She'd surely opted for chance when she showed up without calling first.

Steering her car back down the lane, Kim recalled Beth's warning that Wyatt's shop was a few miles out of the way. Earlier she had suggested her friend come along, but Beth had plans and said Kim would do fine on her own. She'd taken the afternoon off and followed the directions Beth had written on the notepaper, driving past the road twice before spotting the small sign hanging beneath his mailbox. Just as Beth had described, she found the workshop located behind the house. How he'd managed to find something so rural right outside the city limits of Myrtle Beach, South Carolina, was beyond her.

Beth had told her very little about her brother. Kim knew he had to be a few years older than she was, but she couldn't recall how many. The picture she'd seen at Beth's must have been taken years before. Wyatt Alexander looked very different in real life.

His facial features were actually more striking than handsome. A film of dust from the sanding coated his collar-length thick hair, but she could tell it was dark. He wore it combed back, exposing a wide forehead, high cheekbones and a chiseled profile. His sea blue eyes reminded her of the ocean during a storm.

He stood about six feet tall, and his wardrobe consisted of worn jeans and a long-sleeved denim shirt. No doubt about it, Wyatt Alexander had a commanding presence.

Kim wondered if all his clients felt so awkward in his presence or if only she had. From the moment she'd introduced herself, the feeling he didn't want her there had dominated their discussion. Still, a part of her refused to feel anything less than jubilant. She needed a cross, and he had promised to build it for her. That was all that mattered.

❧

What had he just agreed to do? Wyatt brushed his hand

through his hair and knocked loose some of the sanding dust. He needed to remember to lock that door. And fix the front bell.

He'd been startled when he'd glanced up and spotted Kimberly Elliott standing there. She was a tiny thing, not much more than five feet or so, and he doubted she weighed a hundred pounds. She wore her black hair cut short and straight, and those huge green eyes didn't miss a thing.

Why had Beth sent that woman his way? She had to know he wasn't the least bit interested in building a cross. But he also knew his sister worried about his salvation. Other than his parents, he figured she was the only one. God had very little use for an old sinner like him.

He should have said no. But he loved Beth and owed her a great debt. If she wanted him to build a cross for her friend, there was no reason why he couldn't. Maybe it would give Beth a bit of comfort to see the cross standing in the church and know he'd built it with his own two hands.

He pushed the safety goggles back on and reached for the sander. He'd do a good job on the cross to impress his sister. Maybe even his parents. Wyatt's lips curved into a cynical smile as he considered whether or not he should let Kimberly Elliott put his name on the program. Maybe that would show the people at Cornerstone he wasn't all bad. No doubt the tongues would start wagging again the moment they learned the source of their cross.

Would knowing that the troubled Alexander boy had built it make it intolerable for the congregation? Many years ago he'd learned to live with their judgmental ways. Did Kimberly Elliott have any idea what she'd gotten herself into by asking for his help?

two

The bell over the antique mall door jangled, and Kim glanced up from the notes she'd been working on between customers. Pastor Joe had suggested a drama team committee meeting, and she wanted to be prepared.

Her smile broadened at the sight of her pastor's wife who was also her friend. "Mari. Hi. I was just thinking about calling you."

"And here I've saved you all that effort of dialing the phone," she teased.

Two years earlier, after the heartbreak of her last failed relationship and learning her parents wanted to retire early and travel, Kim had returned home to the beach. She hadn't regretted her decision. Renewing relationships with people from her past, coming back to her home church, and making friends with people like Mari Dennis made her happier than she'd been in a long time.

Kim laughed. "If only all my plans worked out so smoothly. Where are the kids?"

"At home with their dad. He volunteered to watch them when I said I planned to come here to look for a gift. Mumbled something about five bulls in a china shop."

No doubt he understood the premise of turning five small children loose in a store as crowded with stuff as Eclectics. Not that they were bad. In fact, the Dennises had some of the best-behaved children Kim knew.

"He's working at home today anyway. He's using that new laptop Julie gave him to write his sermon."

The pastor's sister, Julie, had burst into their lives like a breath of fresh air two weeks before the Christmas holiday. She'd come to care for the Dennises' five children while their parents toured the Holy Land. Kim had met Julie when she brought the older boys to play practice. She liked the young woman immensely and had been happy when Julie and Noah Loughlin, their associate pastor, solved their differences and married on New Year's Eve. Soon Julie would join their congregation, and Kim looked forward to her being there.

"How is she?"

Mari picked up a collector's plate from the counter and looked it over before replacing it carefully. "I hope not as love-sick as Noah. She sent him home after their honeymoon with a promise to follow him here as soon as she packs up and sells her place in Denver. He's been moping around ever since. You should have seen his face when I mentioned finding a birthday gift for her this morning. I hope he realizes she'll never let him forget if he doesn't remember her birthday this year."

"But he won't, thanks to you. You're really in your Good Samaritan mode today. So do you think Julie might like an extra large lion?" Kim chuckled.

The huge garden statuary had stood outside in front of their antique mall ever since her dad had acquired it years ago. Her mother couldn't believe he'd bought it, but over the years it had become a location marker for their store. Directions to Eclectics always included the phrase *with the lion in the parking lot.*

"I don't think she has a use for a large stone lion. Besides, how would anyone find you if you sold that thing?"

"True," Kim acknowledged. "Are you looking for anything in particular?"

"She collects pottery."

Kim shook her head. "Don't have any. I have the card of a local potter who does beautiful work. On the expensive side, though."

Mari sighed. "I'll just wander around and see what I find." She started to walk away and stopped. "What were you going to call me about? Wait—let me guess. The Easter play?" When Kim nodded, she grinned and asked, "How did I know?"

"How could you not? Have I talked about anything else since Pastor Joe told me?"

"You deserve to be excited. Julie was beside herself when Noah told her. She's so glad you asked."

Kim had the pastor's sister to thank for her success. She didn't know whether she would have asked about putting on the play if Julie hadn't encouraged her to try. "I'm pretty excited myself. When Pastor Joe asked me to stop by the office, I just knew he was going to tell me no."

Mari shook her head. "I read the play, Kim. There's no way they could have refused you."

"I want everything to be perfect."

Mari nodded. "And it will be. You have many people dedicated to your success. We believe your play is the beginning of change for Cornerstone."

"Not without struggle, I'm sure. Pastor Joe told me a couple of older board members weren't happy with the decision at first."

"But the others were in full agreement," Mari pointed out, "and soon they all came around. People don't always respond well to change in the beginning, but eventually they understand it's essential to accomplishing the church's goals."

"I know, but I wouldn't want my play to cause problems in the church."

Mari smiled. "Joe and the board members prayed. You prayed. I prayed. This is what God wants."

Kim fiddled with a stack of business cards, arranging them neatly in the holder. "Can you help? I know you have your hands full with the kids, but I could use your talents."

"What did you have in mind?"

"Costumes?"

Mari shrugged. "What sort of budget do we have?"

"The church gave me a couple of hundred dollars, but I plan to supplement that with my own funds."

"There's no need to break the bank," Mari cautioned. "We can look for bargains at the fabric stores. Lots of fabric is wide enough that it probably wouldn't take more than a yard for each child."

"Thanks, Mari."

"I'm as excited as you are. I know the message will be even more poignant with the children performing the roles."

"I want Matt as a disciple. He already has the perfect name for the role. Too bad Mark, Luke, and John are too little."

Mari looked doubtful. "I'm afraid Matt's a bit young."

"He can handle it."

Mari wasn't convinced. "We saw the video of the Christmas play. Our boys wreaked havoc in that program."

"Luke did steal the show," Kim agreed. "But it was my fault for giving him a live lamb as a prop. I plan to keep Matt's role simple. One speaking line and some walk-on scenes."

"If you're sure. By the way, Julie says to tell you she has a million ideas and can't wait to get here to help."

Kim giggled. "You gotta love that woman. Noah says she takes planning to new heights."

"I don't know what she has in mind but, knowing Julie as I do, she'll jump right in. I'd better see what I can find. Joe will be wondering what happened to me."

"Take your time," Kim said. "It'll make him appreciate how hard you really work."

Mari walked away with a smile, and Kim thought back to the day she'd approached Pastor Joe with the Easter play she'd had published. He had been very complimentary and congratulated her on her writing success. He'd asked to read the play before he presented it to the board. She'd come prepared and handed over copies of the program before leaving the church office.

Kim had experienced a sinking feeling in the pit of her stomach the following morning when she'd answered the phone and recognized the pastor's voice. She just knew he wanted to let her down gently. But the news had been good. She still couldn't believe they were allowing her to produce *Except for Grace*.

"Can you stop by the office?" Pastor Joe had said.

"Sure. Any time in particular?"

"I'll be here all day."

"See you around lunchtime then."

The butterflies in her stomach hadn't allowed her to consider food. Kim had driven to the church and gone straight to the office. Joe Dennis had greeted her and invited her to have a seat.

"First, I wanted to say I'm humbled by what I read. You definitely have talent."

"Thanks, Pastor Joe."

"I'm serious, Kim. Your play is incredible. The renewal I felt was too tremendous for words. I immediately asked Mari to read it, and when she agreed I contacted the board to ask them to consider the matter. Since then, the two board members who read it promptly recommended it to the others. It's excellent. I mean. . ." Pastor Joe had paused then said, "Well, the story moved me to renew my faith."

His words had sent a chill down her spine. She'd felt the same way as the words appeared on her computer screen, almost seeming to write themselves.

"Two members hesitated at first, but then the entire board voted unanimously to allow you to produce your play for Easter. They even suggested we advertise."

Kim had gawked. "You're kidding."

Pastor Joe had shaken his head. "No, I'm not. After I described how it renewed my spiritual foundation, they all wanted copies. I've received so many positive comments. I hope you don't mind."

"What? Hearing my work complimented?" Kim had asked with a trill of laughter. "Bring it on. I think I can handle all you can give and more." Her careless repartee had struck Kim as prideful, and she'd felt instant remorse. "I'm sorry. That was facetious, and you're serious."

"I understand, Kim. I know you're excited."

She had nodded slowly, feeling her eyes moisten. "I've prayed over it. Several times, in fact. I so wanted Cornerstone to do something of mine. But I was afraid to ask. If it hadn't been for Julie. . ."

Pastor Joe's expression had grown curious. "What does my sister have to do with this?"

"She encouraged me to come to you with the play."

He had smiled. "Thank the Lord she did. I have a feeling about this program. It's going to be quite an Easter celebration around here this year. Did you hear the Good Shepherd window will be dedicated on Easter morning?"

"That's wonderful!" Kim had exclaimed. "I can't wait to see it in place."

"God is truly blessing Cornerstone this year."

Overwhelmed, Kim hadn't been able to speak and only nodded. Silently she had prayed God would indeed use her as one of His disciples.

Mari drew her back to the present when she laid some items on the counter.

Kim smiled at her. "Did you find something for Julie?"

"No, but I found plenty for myself."

Eclectics was exactly what the name implied, a mixture of just about anything a person could want. The store itself covered nearly an acre and contained furniture—antique and used, books, records, jewelry, bric-a-brac, glass, dishes, rugs, and yard ornaments. She bought some items outright, then worked with the owners on commission for other things.

Mari had chosen a carved wooden box, a tiny pink glass rooster, and a couple of books. As Kim wrote up the paperwork and wrapped the items, they talked about getting together soon.

"I could use a girls' night out," Mari said. "It's hard to believe it's only been three weeks since we got back from vacation. I want to show you our photos."

"I can't wait to see them. Will Julie be here in time for our night out?"

"She told Noah she's packing the condo now. They had some good news, too. When she turned in her two weeks' notice, her boss said she's too valuable to lose. He wants her to continue her computer troubleshooting work from here and travel to Denver as needed. I think Noah and Julie are both very happy she won't have to look for work."

"That is good news. I'm so eager for her to get here. If she hadn't encouraged me, I'd never have had the nerve to approach Pastor Joe. I kept thinking I shouldn't rock the boat."

"I'm looking forward to having her here, too," Mari said. "She's the sister I never had. Joe's a bit worried that she's going to shake things up at Cornerstone."

"I'm sure she'll fit right in."

Mari glanced at the antique clock on the counter. "I need to run. I'll be in touch to make plans."

"Talk to you soon. Tell Pastor Joe and the children hello for me."

"I will," Mari said, waving good-bye as she walked out the door.

three

After work Kim drove straight to the hardware store to buy the landscape timbers. The salesperson directed her to an outside display. As she studied the long poles, she could see why Wyatt thought they'd make a good cross. She picked through the lot, choosing the more battered pieces. It took a bit of finagling to load them into her sedan, and then she set off for Wyatt's.

She parked and got out. Where was the dog? She walked over to find a CLOSED sign on the door. Great. What was she supposed to do with the two eight-foot poles sticking out of her trunk? Kim thought she heard the whine of power tools inside and tried to look in the window. *Could he be here? Only one way to find out.*

She knocked on the door. When there was no answer, she knocked again and shouted his name loudly.

She should have called first. Walking back to the car, Kim considered what to do. Maybe she could leave the timbers by the building if she could get them out of the car. She started to untie the cord.

"I'm closed."

Kim whirled around. "Hi."

Wyatt seemed a bit surprised by her presence. "What are you doing here?"

"I brought the timbers. I wanted to make sure you had them when you're ready to start work."

He used his pocketknife to cut the cord and pulled the poles from the trunk. "Good thing your seats fold down, or you'd never have gotten these in here."

Wyatt hefted one onto his shoulder and carried it to the building.

"I thought you'd gone home for the day."

When he returned for the other one, Kim followed him inside. She noticed the floor was covered with wood shavings from the piece on the workbench. "What are you working on?"

"A fireplace surround for a house in Charleston. I have a lot to do. They want it next week."

Kim studied the workmanship of the piece. "This is gorgeous."

"I'm trying to replicate some unusual trim in the house. It's kind of tricky."

She traced her finger along the smooth wood then walked over to study the carving on an armoire. She glanced at him. "You did this?"

"It's all my work."

"I'm impressed. I can see why Beth says you're the best."

He didn't say anything as he picked up the carving tool and continued the project he'd been working on.

"I'm excited about the cross. I know you'll do a fantastic job."

Wyatt grunted.

"I've been working on my to-do list today," Kim said. "I still can't believe they're going to let me do the play." Again he didn't speak. "Did you ever attend Cornerstone?" she asked.

"When I was younger."

His answer encouraged Kim to ask another question. "Why not now? Beth and your parents are there all the time."

Wyatt dropped the carving tool on the counter and faced her. "Look. I'm busy here. And as for Cornerstone, that's none of your business. I'll get to the cross as soon as I can. I'll let Beth know when it's ready."

Kim reached into her coat pocket. "Here's the store card. You can reach me there during the day."

"I'll call you."

Kim quickly said good-bye. "I'll lock up after myself."

❧

When only the scent of her perfume lingered, Wyatt wondered why he'd let her stay as long as he had. Why hadn't he told her he was busy instead of listening to her prattle? Maybe because he found Kimberly Elliott interesting, even entertaining at times. She was the first woman he'd ever met who could talk a mile a minute without stopping for breath.

And if he told the truth, she wasn't bad to look at either; but his sister's little friend was out of his league. All that was left for him was his shop and life as he knew it. He'd secured his fate all those years ago when he'd decided to drink and drive.

❧

After leaving Wyatt's, Kim hurried through her grocery shopping and headed home. She wanted to work on her planning but knew she had to do laundry if she intended to shower and wear clean clothes. She'd used the last towel in the linen closet that morning.

Maybe she could work on the notes over dinner. She'd picked up some frozen microwave meals. Not that she minded cooking, but preparing a meal for one seemed senseless.

After she put the laundry in the dryer, Kim went into the kitchen and placed her dinner in the microwave. She prepared a small salad and poured some flavored bottled water into a glass before settling in at the table with a legal pad and pen.

She made notes as she ate, listing the character parts she could recall. She'd need to do a more detailed list later that included the walk-ons. For now, the key player would be Jesus.

It definitely required someone who would carry through with the commitment, someone capable of learning the lines. And since a child would play the role she needed supportive parents who would guarantee the child's presence at practice.

Kim listed the boys who fell in the ten-, eleven-, and twelve-year-old age range. She marked through several of them immediately, knowing they'd never be willing to devote so much time to the play.

Chase. She smiled as she jotted down the name. Perfect. The twelve-year-old was tall for his age, well mannered, and one of the few children she knew who respected his elders. She'd seen his interaction with Beth enough to know that. And having an aunt who was active in church would help ensure he carried through on his commitment.

She grabbed the cordless phone and dialed Beth's number. "Hi, have I interrupted your dinner?"

"I picked up burgers. Chase is studying for a math exam. How was work?"

"Slow. Mari stopped by. She's going to help sew costumes for the play."

"I'm so happy they said yes," Beth said. "When you mentioned you were going to talk to Pastor Dennis, I figured they were so anchored to tradition they'd never consider anything but the cantata."

"I thought the same," Kim admitted. "When Pastor Joe called me to the office and said yes, I nearly fainted. I've been singing God's praises ever since."

"I'm thrilled," Beth told her. "That play deserves to be seen."

"Thanks. That's why I'm calling. Do you think Chase would take on the role of Jesus? I know it's a major commitment, but I'd help him any way I can. We'd only practice once a week up until a couple of weeks before Good Friday, and then we'd probably have a few extra rehearsals. What do you think?"

"Why don't you come over and ask him?"

"But he's studying," Kim said.

"He's due a break. I just fixed a snack for him."

Beth and Chase lived in the condominium next door to hers. For now, it was just Beth and Chase. Beth's husband of three years, Gerald Erikson, was overseas in the military.

"I'll be right there."

Kim turned off the dryer and grabbed her keys before leaving the house. Multistoried, their second-floor condominiums opened onto a breezeway that fronted the parking lot. She stepped around the divider wall and rang the doorbell, smiling at Chase when he appeared in the doorway.

The boy's broad smile reminded her of someone. "Hey, Miss Kim."

Probably Beth, Kim thought as she stepped inside. "Hey, Chase. How's the studying going?"

"Pretty good. It's math. I'm good at that," he said with an air of confidence.

Kim knew the child had won math and science awards at school. "Did your aunt Beth tell you I was coming over?"

He shook his head. "I answered the door on my way to the kitchen."

The condos were designed with two bedrooms and a bathroom near the entry door. A hallway led to the galley kitchen and combination dining/living room, with the master bedroom and bath off to the side. Balconies fronted the building, looking out onto the beach.

Kim indicated he should lead the way. "I hear there's a snack waiting. Don't let me keep you."

They found Beth in the living room, crocheting as she watched television. "Your snack's on the counter, Chase. There's a cup of cocoa for you, too, Kim."

She picked up the cup and went to sit down next to Beth. "What are you making?"

"A tablecloth." Beth spread out the work she'd done. The pineapple design was detailed.

"It's beautiful. Granny tried to teach me. I couldn't catch on."

"God gave you other talents. Speaking of which"—Beth tilted her head toward Chase—"did you ask him yet?"

"Let him eat first."

"I'm so excited for you," Beth said. "And for Cornerstone. It'll be a wonderful first for everyone."

Kim felt the heat creep up her cheeks. The opportunity thrilled her, but the praise of her work took some getting used to. "I just pray I can carry it through to give God the glory."

"You know you can. Didn't God give you the talent and the idea?"

"He did. To tell you the truth, I'm more thrilled by Cornerstone saying yes than I was when the editor bought the program."

Beth looked doubtful. "I seem to recall you bouncing off the walls for several days after getting that news."

"That was pretty exciting, too," she admitted with a grin.

"And now you get to see it performed."

"I finished studying my math," Chase announced. "Can I watch television?"

Beth glanced at the clock. "Until eight thirty. Then you need to take your shower and get into bed. You want to be rested tomorrow."

"Yes, ma'am."

"Before you go, Miss Kim has something to ask you."

The feeling she'd seen that expression before hit her again when he looked at her. "This year Cornerstone has agreed to produce the Easter play I wrote. The main character in the play is Jesus, and I wondered if you'd consider taking on the role." When the boy didn't say anything right away, Kim added, "I don't want to pressure you, but it would mean a great deal to me and the church."

"But soccer practice starts soon." He looked at Beth. "You promised I could play if I kept my grades up."

"We'd only practice one night a week in the beginning," Kim promised. "I'll work with you on memorizing the lines and such."

"Can I think about it?"

"Of course. I want you to pray about your decision, Chase." She glanced at Beth and back at the boy. "The main thing is, this is our chance to do something good for Jesus. People who don't know Him as their Savior will attend the play, and I'm praying the message will touch their hearts and help them realize they need Jesus in their lives."

The boy nodded. "I'll let you know."

Kim smiled at him. "That's all I can ask."

After Chase left the room, Kim looked at Beth. "Think I can compete with soccer practice?"

"Maybe. Chase has a strong sense of service to God. He's the child who always wants to do good no matter what his friends say."

"Thank the Lord for that. You're certainly blessed."

Her friend nodded. "So tell me about Wyatt," Beth said. "I imagine he was surprised to see you."

Kim considered that an understatement. "He wasn't very enthusiastic about my request. At first he said no, but then he agreed to build a cross using landscape timbers and some scrap from his business."

"Did you tell him I sent you?"

"And that you said he's the best carpenter you know," Kim added. "He said you had to say that because you're his sister. Is he always so gruff?"

Beth laughed. "Wyatt can be difficult at times. When did you see him?"

"Yesterday and again today. He told me to bring over landscape timbers, and I figured the sooner the better. I took them after work. The building was locked up tight, but he opened the door just before I was about to leave."

"He puts in lots of hours," Beth said. "He's always deep into some project or another. I can't say the last time he attended a family gathering."

"He was working on a very detailed fireplace surround today. Said it has to be completed by next week."

"He's a true artisan. I just wish he had more of a life."

Kim sipped her cocoa. "This is good." The wind rattled the chimes on the deck. "Sounds like there's another weather change on the way."

"The winds are blowing in colder air. The weather report says the high will be in the thirties tomorrow."

Kim pulled her sweater closer at the thought of another chilly day at the beach. "I think I antagonized Wyatt when I asked why he doesn't attend Cornerstone. He told me it was none of my business."

Beth winced and concentrated on pulling more string from the ball. "He used to go. Back when he was married to Karen. It's a tragic story." Sadness etched lines in Beth's expression. "Wyatt's turning away from God has been a burden on my heart for years." She lowered her voice as she spoke. "That and the fact that he's separated himself from Chase."

Kim felt as if Beth had handed her yet another piece of the puzzle, but she had no idea where it went.

"I'm not sure he ever truly believed," Beth continued.

"But he attended church," Kim said.

"Because our parents forced him to go. I suppose Daddy thought if he could get him there God would do the rest. Wyatt told me once he wanted no part of Daddy's religion. It's difficult to believe in a forgiving God when your Christian role model is your harshest judge." Beth sighed heavily. "And even tougher being young and foolish and having your face rubbed in your every mistake, particularly when your father is the one doing the rubbing. I thought things had improved after Wyatt married Karen and Chase was born. Wyatt seemed to settle down."

A vague image teased Kim's thoughts—that of a withdrawn older boy who always seemed unhappy. Everything fell into place. How could she have forgotten him? All those years ago Wyatt Alexander had become the role model of "what not to do with your life" to more than one parent at Cornerstone. She'd been twelve to his sixteen, and, despite her parents' efforts to shelter her, rumors of Wyatt's exploits had circulated throughout the church youth. Kim remembered that he hung out with a tough crowd and drank, and then he'd gotten his girlfriend pregnant. She recalled the baby being born about the time she'd gone off to college.

"What changed him?" Why was she so curious about Wyatt Alexander?

Beth glanced toward the bedroom, listening for the sound of Chase's television before she continued. "Wyatt and Karen went to a party one night when Chase was just under two. They had too much to drink, and there was an accident on the way home. Not their fault—a large truck tire shredded on the interstate, and Wyatt rolled the car. Karen was thrown from the vehicle and died instantly. The car ended up against a concrete piling, and Wyatt was pinned inside. They had to use the Jaws of Life to cut him free."

"That's awful."

Beth nodded. "After the truth came out about their drinking, Daddy really came down hard on Wyatt. Told him he wasn't fit to be a father. Wyatt agreed. He left Chase with them. I always believed he'd come to his senses and take Chase home, but he didn't. Our parents aren't young people, and as their health worsened, taking care of Chase became more difficult for them. I agreed to become his guardian. When Gerald and I started dating, he didn't mind, and we agreed to remain as Chase's guardians after we were married. He loves Chase, too."

"He's a lovable child," Kim agreed. "But I don't understand how Wyatt could abandon his son."

"Wyatt was badly injured in the accident. I know people don't understand, but he's doing what he thinks best for

Chase. I have to respect that, but Chase knows Wyatt is his father."

"Why not just let you adopt him and never tell the child?"

"I wouldn't want that. And neither would Chase. He may not understand his father, but he's entitled to know the truth about his family. I'm praying that one day he and Wyatt can form a father-son bond and put the past behind them. Meanwhile I'll ensure he has a safe, loving home."

"What about when you and Gerald decide to have children of your own? Won't Chase feel out of place?"

Beth shook her head. "If Wyatt doesn't make a decision soon, I'll ask to formally adopt Chase." The television clicked off, and she glanced at the clock. "It's his bedtime."

Kim stood. "Let me go so you can get him settled for the night."

Beth took the mug and set it in the sink. They hugged and walked toward the door. Beth stopped by Chase's room and said, "Miss Kim is leaving."

He came to stand in the door. " 'Night, Miss Kim."

She touched his cheek. " 'Night, honey. Sleep well."

When she opened the door to leave, he called her name. She looked at him. "About the play. . . ," he began. "I'd like to play Jesus."

"Think about it a day or so," she encouraged him. "I don't have to know right away."

"But what you said about helping those people. You mean like my dad, right?"

Kim glanced at Beth then reached to hug Chase. "God works in His own time, and I can't say who the play will help. It could be a complete stranger. Or it could be no one."

"But it could be my dad," he said. "I want to help, Miss Kim."

"You will. You have a good heart, Chase Alexander. Let's talk about this at church on Sunday, and if you still feel you want to take the role I'd love to have you portray Jesus." He nodded. "Pray about it. It's a major commitment."

"I will," he declared solemnly.

Kim winked at him. "And I'll pray that you ace that math test tomorrow."

He smiled, and she knew exactly where she'd seen that smile before—lurking in the corners of Wyatt Alexander's mouth.

four

Pastor Joe rapped on the podium, and the chattering stopped as heads turned to where the pastor stood. "We appreciate everyone coming to this meeting. We thought it would be a good idea to meet and determine where everyone can help with the Easter program.

"First thing, though, I have a prayer request from Mrs. Allene Rogers. As most of you are aware, Mrs. Allene has been ill for some time now. The doctors officially diagnosed her with cancer this morning." Several gasps echoed about the room. "I know all of us will keep her in our prayers. I don't want to put a damper on our Easter celebration plans, but it's important we pray now."

After they lifted their heads Pastor Joe turned the meeting over to Kim.

She smiled as she moved to the podium. "Thank you so much for being here. It means a lot to me. Tonight I'd like to share a list of needs and see where everyone's interests lie. First of all, we'll need some stones."

"I'd like to make them," Avery Baker said.

"Sounds like fun," Natalie Porter said.

Kim saw the resentment in Avery's eyes when he looked at Natalie. The standing rivalry between the two was old news at the church.

Avery Baker owned the local bakery. Natalie Porter had come to the area a couple of years before when a heart attack forced her to step away from the hectic lifestyle she'd lived in New York. Since her arrival Natalie had made a name for herself with the delicious creative cakes she made in her home, and Avery refused to see her as anything but the competition.

"Okay if I put you both down for that project?" Kim asked, not surprised by Avery's grudging nod.

"Great. For now we need sufficient kids at practice to fill the roles. Chase Alexander is the most important since he's agreed to play Jesus. The disciple roles are still in limbo. I may have to use some of the older girls."

"Wouldn't this have been easier with adults?" Geneva Simpson asked.

"Certainly," Kim answered. "But I have two main reasons for a children's performance. The first is that I'm praying a little child will lead them. The parents of a number of our children do not attend services. It says a lot that Cornerstone's children's outreach program is so strong, but I'm praying their parents will come for the play and want to come back.

"My second reason is that I feel it's important the children play a role in the Easter celebration. The adult choir has the cantata on Palm Sunday, but there's very little for the children and youth beyond the egg hunt. We all know the statistics regarding children and how important it is to involve them in church while they're young."

Several members of the group nodded, and Kim continued. "I have a list of what we need volunteers to do. The church budgeted two hundred dollars, and Mari has been searching the fabric stores for inexpensive material. Wyatt Alexander has agreed to build our cross for the cost of materials only."

The puzzled expressions on the older members' faces took Kim by surprise. "I'm sure he'll do an excellent job. He does beautiful work at his woodworking business."

"Where does he attend church?" Pastor Joe asked.

Kim swallowed hard. "Nowhere actually. Beth Erikson and I were talking about carpenters, and she told me her brother's the best. I didn't want to leave our cross to the last minute, so

I approached Wyatt, and he agreed."

"Good idea," Pastor Joe said with a smile and a nod. "God needs more workers, and perhaps we can encourage Mr. Alexander to attend the program."

"Ah, pastor, he's Wilbur and Kay Alexander's son," Burris Simmons volunteered. "There's some history there."

"We all have history, Burris. I look forward to thanking Mr. Alexander for his help."

Kim suspected the Alexanders had talked with Pastor Joe about their son. "Actually he doesn't want any recognition."

Pastor Joe's nod indicated his understanding. "Go ahead, Kim."

"I was thinking we need a platform for the pulpit area. To raise the children high enough to be seen."

"I'll ask for lumber donations at prayer meeting tomorrow night," the pastor said, jotting a note on his pad.

Kim smiled her thanks. "We won't have stage curtains, so everything will need to be set up before the scenes unfold. I have pewter trays and goblets at the store, so unless they sell before Easter I'll provide those. If they sell, I'll replace them with something else."

She read from the list. "We need fabric and trim and seamstresses. Costumes for disciples, crowds, soldiers, angels—and white robes for Jesus."

Mari raised her hand. Kim called on her.

"I devised a rough pattern for some of the regular costumes last night. I had a flat full-sized white sheet and got two costumes out of one sheet. We can dye them in various colors and use a macramé cord around their waists for belts."

"Excellent idea," Kim said. "That's the sort of creativity we need. I'm sure I have a couple of flat sheets I never use. Only the key characters' costumes need to be fancy. Shoes can be any kind of sandal. We need greenery for the garden. And the stones. Preferably a lightweight version."

Mari raised her hand again. "I picked up a pattern for those fancier costumes today."

"So we need to come up with a final number of participants?"

Mari nodded. "And then later we can have a work night to finalize the costumes and props."

Kim added that to her list and continued with her notes. "I can't begin to tell you all how important it is to work with the children whose parents don't attend. We'll be seeking a major commitment from each child and will need to do our part to help them carry through."

"That means the bus will need to pick up children on practice nights," Noah said.

"I thought we might plan practice nights to coordinate with children's church over in the fellowship hall. Closer to the actual performance we'd need to bring them in more regularly, but we can deal with that later."

"What about music and sound effects?" Rob, their music minister, asked.

"We need soft music to play between scenes. And sound effects like thunder and driving nails."

"And a crowing rooster," he said. "I have a sound effects CD."

Kim scribbled another note. "Some children have beautiful voices, and I'd like to incorporate their talent into the play. I'm sure we all remember Missy Reynolds's rendition of 'Away in a Manger' at Christmas. It would be a shame not to utilize that talent. My plan is to include every child who wants to be a part of *Except for Grace*. It will mean adding roles as we go, but if a child wants to be in the play I feel he or she should be.

"I also thought we might have refreshments afterward. Nothing fancy—cake and punch, nuts, that sort of thing."

Natalie raised her hand. "I'll donate a cake."

"Me, too," Avery said. "And some cookies."

Kim jotted their names in her notes. "Wonderful. Have I forgotten anything?"

"What about using a grapevine to make the crown of thorns?" someone suggested.

Another hand shot up. "I have that machine that puts studs and eyelets in fabric. We can use that for the soldiers' costumes."

The ideas flew back and forth for several minutes, and Kim wrote rapidly, not wanting to miss anything. Not only did she plan to involve the children, but she also wanted the adults to feel they were part of the process.

"We've made some definite progress. Oh, angel wings. We need angel wings."

Everyone laughed at her last-minute addition.

"I'll be responsible for those," Natalie said. "How many angels?"

"At least three. Does that include the costume?"

"Sure," Natalie agreed. "Does white satin with gold cording sound okay?"

"Perfect," Kim declared, scribbling Natalie's name on her sheet. "At the risk of repeating myself, I can't tell you all how much I appreciate your help."

"I think I speak for everyone when I say how delighted we are to have this opportunity," Pastor Joe agreed. "All our volunteers will need to report to Kim. Let her know if you have donations."

"I'll ask the senior ladies' sewing guild about the costumes," Mari offered. "I'm sure they'd love to participate."

Kim nodded. "I plan to check back with everyone, and you have my number at the store and at home if you need to contact me. I'm honored that Cornerstone has shown such faith in me. I intend to give it my all."

After the meeting the group members chatted among themselves. Kim looked around when Maggie touched her arm and smiled at her friend. "I'll do everything I can to help, but I can't commit completely because of my schedule and Mrs. Allene."

"I understand," Kim told her. Mrs. Allene had brought Maggie Gregory into their midst about ten years before when Maggie moved into Mrs. Allene's rental property. Since Kim's return to the beach, their friendship had developed, and she considered Maggie one of her best friends. "I'm so sorry about Mrs. Allene. Didn't they have any idea?"

Maggie shook her head. "I went to the doctor's office with her. The doctor seemed as shocked as we were."

"Did they say how bad it is?"

"He said maybe six months if she agrees to treatment. Why didn't I make her go sooner?"

"You didn't know," Kim said, hoping to offer her some comfort.

"I'm a registered nurse. I knew something was wrong, but I let her convince me it was only the aches and pains of old age."

"Who will take care of her? Will she have to go into a home?"

"I'm considering requesting a leave of absence."

"Will the hospital allow you to do that?"

"I've worked for them for years and taken very little time off. I would think they'd give me this leave."

Kim nodded, thinking how selfless Maggie's action was.

"Mrs. Allene does have a son. I've been trying to get her to call him. She said she would once she knew what was wrong. Will you go over with me after the meeting and see if we can convince her to make the call?"

"Sure," Kim agreed readily.

"I'm glad you asked Wyatt to build the cross. He built my television armoire. I found his shop one day and couldn't resist."

"Your armoire is gorgeous." She hesitated then let out a breath. "Wyatt Alexander is a very complex man."

"What are you thinking, Kim?"

"Nothing."

"Please tell me you're not attracted to him."

Kim looked away. "You know I promised not to get involved with another man who would hurt me in the end."

"I'm not sure you can help yourself. You heard Burris. The man has issues."

"I didn't need him to tell me that. I knew that from talking to Wyatt."

"Be careful, Kim. You know your heart."

"And I remember the vow I made to God. I will not end up the loser in yet another relationship. This is ridiculous. I've met the man twice."

"I can tell by the look on your face that there's already more to this than meets the eye."

"Beth confided a bit of their past to me—most I'd forgotten."

"I know some of his history, too, having moved here soon after his wife died." Maggie frowned.

"I told you there's nothing to it," Kim said, trying to assure her friend—and herself. "Let's finish up here and go over to see Mrs. Allene."

five

After their visit to Mrs. Allene's, Kim drove home, parked in her space, and took the elevator to her second-story unit. The chill of the night encouraged her to walk faster along the open walkway. She rounded the corner to her doorway and screamed when she nearly ran into a man.

"Hello, Kim."

"Wyatt? Did you come to visit Beth and Chase?"

"They're not home."

Kim had phoned Beth earlier to tell her about the drama committee meeting. "She went to check on your mom. She's not feeling well."

Wyatt's brows drew together slightly as he handed Kim an envelope. "Would you give her this for me?"

"Sure. Did you want to come in for a soda or something and wait a few minutes to see if they come home?"

"No, it's late. I need to be getting home."

"We had a meeting tonight about the play," Kim said before he could walk away. "Everyone is pleased you're building the cross."

"It's nothing."

"It most certainly is!" Kim exclaimed. "The cross is precious. Jesus died there for us."

Wyatt held up his hands and took a step back. "Whoa. Maybe making that cross is beyond my capabilities."

"I don't think so. Our Lord was a carpenter as well."

Wyatt shrugged. "You had a late meeting," he said, abruptly changing the subject.

"Not really. Maggie and I went over to see Allene Rogers and try to talk her into calling her son. She's been diagnosed with cancer, and it's bad. She told us to mind our own business."

"I remember Mrs. Rogers. She was my Sunday school teacher years ago. Nice lady."

"Did you know her son?"

"Dillon Rogers is older, closer to my parents' age. I was a kid when he left for overseas."

Kim pushed her purse back up on her shoulder and longed for her gloves in the nippy night air. "I wish someone could make her understand she needs to let him know."

"Obviously she has her reasons. I think you should honor her request and stay out of the situation."

"Her son needs to be here for her," Kim said. "Family is important. How would you feel if something like this happened to your parents and they didn't tell you?"

"I'd think they had their reasons."

She couldn't believe he could be so coldhearted. "I don't think that would be the case at all."

"Stop trying to figure me out, Kim."

"I'm not. I just don't believe you'd turn your back on your parents in their time of need."

"Take it from me, Kim. Not everyone wants to be saved. I'm comfortable in my skin, and I am what I am. I don't need a crusader."

"But you'd be so much happier if you—"

"Let it go," Wyatt interrupted forcefully as he started down the landing to the elevator. "You have no idea what's better for me. No idea at all."

"I know Chase is your son." She clamped her hand over her mouth as the words slipped out.

"Why doesn't that surprise me?" he asked, the question laced with sarcasm.

"Beth is my friend."

"Didn't you ever wonder why she hasn't discussed this with

you before now? Maybe because you didn't remember her wayward brother and now she feels the need to explain me?"

"Beth's not like that. She just can't understand her older brother."

Wyatt shrugged again. "What's to understand? I'm doing the best I can."

"Chase needs to be part of your life. You're his father."

"I'm the man who killed his mother."

"But Beth said—"

"The accident wasn't my fault," he filled in. "I know, but if I hadn't been drinking that night I wouldn't have been so careless. I wouldn't have rolled that car and killed Karen."

"Do you think you're the only person to blame yourself, Wyatt? We all have things we could have done differently."

"What did you do?" he demanded. "Choose the wrong nail polish color once in your life?"

"That's cruel."

"I'm a bad man, Kim. I abandoned my child after I killed his mother."

"Bad man." His words flashed into Kim's head, reminding her of Maggie's warning and her own vow to God. Unable to help herself, she said, "Because you felt that was best for him."

"Obviously Beth didn't share the entire sordid story."

"She said you were badly injured."

"That's an understatement. I lost my foot in the accident. I didn't know if I'd ever walk again. Chase didn't deserve to be burdened with a crippled father."

"He's a very caring child. He wouldn't resent you."

"Thanks to Beth and my parents. I suppose God knows right. The path Karen and I were on would have destroyed him. What kind of life would he have had with two free spirits as parents?"

"Beth said you attended church when you were married."

"Do you want to know why we went to church?" The self-loathing in his tone spoke volumes. "So we could pick up Chase after he'd spent the weekend with my family while we partied. Showing up for preaching kept them off our backs and stopped their sermons about our lives of sin. We were so good at hiding things that on those Sundays when we were so hung over we couldn't attend church, my parents figured we had to be sick. We were masters of illusion until everything fell apart."

"But you've changed."

"Have I?" he asked with a slight smile of defiance. "Like I said, I don't need a savior. Stay out of my business."

&

Later that night Kim lay in bed, unable to sleep as she considered Maggie's shock when Mrs. Allene told them to mind their own business.

Outside Mrs. Allene's house, she'd seen tears in her friend's eyes. "She knows you have her best interests at heart. I'm sure she didn't mean to hurt you."

"I know, but I don't want her to wait too long. He's overseas, and I'm sure he'd need to get things in order and request a leave of absence from work."

"Pray about it, Maggie. I will, too. Mrs. Allene needs time to adjust to the news. Cancer is scary business."

Maggie nodded. "That's why she should be surrounded by people who love her."

"She will be. She has her extended family—you and all the members of Cornerstone. And, the truth be told, you've probably been there for her more than her son over the years."

Kim's thoughts turned then to her own shock when Wyatt warned her to stay out of his business. His words lingered, and his attitude still stung. She didn't need him warning her to stay clear of his bad-boy persona. She remembered again her promise to God.

Perhaps she'd gone too far in her efforts to make him see her side of the story. He resented her sudden involvement in his life, and Kim could understand why. She'd said things she'd never have said if she hadn't been so stirred up over Mrs. Allene and Maggie.

Learning Wyatt had lost a foot was disturbing. Beth hadn't mentioned that. It certainly made his almost-hermit nature more clear. No doubt he preferred keeping to himself rather than dealing with people's sympathy.

Kim closed her eyes and sought God in prayer, asking her heavenly Father to soften Wyatt's heart and open Mrs. Allene's eyes to the need to call her son. She prayed for Maggie and then asked God to forgive her for the attack on Wyatt. She owed Wyatt Alexander an apology.

six

Business filled the next few days. When sales picked up, Kim suspected everyone had finished packing away their holiday decorations and wanted something new to brighten their homes.

Kim found herself exhausted by the time she arrived home each evening. She'd talked with her parents the day before, and they had promised to be home for Easter. Her mother was more excited than Kim. "Just imagine," her mom had said, "I'll be able to tell everyone my daughter, the playwright, is producing her program."

She laughed at her mother's statement. "That's a little grandiose for a church production, don't you think?"

"I've always been proud of your talent."

"I know." At times her mother's bragging embarrassed Kim.

"So bring me up to date on what's happening at the beach."

The news of Mrs. Allene's cancer stunned her mother.

"Give me her number. I'd like to call her."

Kim found the church directory and flipped to the *R*'s. Mrs. Allene's smiling face flashed before her, and pain hit Kim at the thought of not having the elderly woman in her life. She recited the number. "We're praying for her."

"I'll certainly do the same. She's always been such a vibrant woman."

"I think this illness has affected her. I went with Maggie to talk to her, and she got really upset when we urged her to call her son home."

"Where is Dillon? Still in Saudi Arabia?"

"Somewhere like that," Kim agreed. "I can understand her

not wanting to be a burden to him, but I know how I'd feel if it were you or Daddy. She has so many decisions to make. It breaks my heart."

"You can't force her to do something she doesn't want to do, Kim."

"But don't you think he'd want her to call him?"

"I'm sure she will. Once she's ready. I'm sure she needs to get herself together first. Parents have to stay strong for their children."

Kim hadn't considered that. "I miss you and Daddy."

"We miss you, too, sweetie, but we're enjoying our stay in Sedona. You should see this place. RVs everywhere you look."

"Has Daddy played golf?"

"Are you kidding? I have to pry the clubs out of his hands every night."

Kim loved her mother's sense of humor. "Are you playing, too?"

"Only when he can't find someone else. And I never argue about being left behind."

Her mother had never cared for the game. At home in Myrtle Beach, Kim's father had played every opportunity he had, and with the number of courses in the area that opportunity was around the corner all year long.

The only time her mother had objected to his golfing was when some of his business associates wanted to play on Sunday mornings. She'd insisted the Lord had blessed him far too much for him not to attend church.

Her father argued he could worship God just as well during a golf game while breathing the fresh air as he could on a hard pew in church. Her mother disagreed, so later on Sunday afternoon her dad would usually disappear for a few rounds.

"Why do you suppose he never pursued golf professionally?" Kim asked the question she'd often wondered about.

"Maybe out of fear he couldn't support a family. At least

he's been able to take early retirement and golf to his heart's content. Enough of that. I called to talk about you. Congratulations again, Kimmie. I knew you could do it."

"God did it, Mom. Those words aren't mine. They're His. He deserves all the glory. I'm honored to serve as His vessel."

"That's my girl. Love you bunches."

"Love you, too, Mom. Give Daddy my love. And be sure to include the church in your prayers. It's going to take a major collaboration to carry this off."

"Honey, you know we'll be praying for you and the church. And I'll send you a little something to help with the budget."

"You don't have to," Kim told her. "I'm adding to what the church gave me."

"A bit more won't hurt."

Kim started to say good night and then asked, "Mom, do you remember Wyatt Alexander?"

"Wilbur and Kay Alexander's son?"

"Yes. What do you remember about him?"

"Kay's had the women of the church praying for him for years. Why do you ask?"

"I met him recently. He's building the cross for the play. He does beautiful cabinetry work. I'm thinking of asking him to redo my kitchen."

"Renovation is expensive. You should get a couple of quotes before you decide on a contractor," her mother advised.

"I know he'd do a good job."

"I'm sure he would, but cover all your bases. Good night, Kim."

She hung up and started when the phone rang again immediately. Perhaps her mother had forgotten something. "Mom?"

"Wyatt Alexander here. I called to tell you your cross is nearly finished. I thought maybe you could stop by and tell me whether it's what you wanted."

He sounded so dispassionate. Kim cautioned herself to restrain her excitement. "Sure. When?"

"Wednesday evening?"

"Right after work. We have play practice afterward, so I'll be able to tell the kids about the cross."

"See you Wednesday then."

"Definitely. And thanks, Wyatt."

"It's nothing."

She didn't argue the point, but Kim definitely felt it was a step in the right direction. Anyone who would build a cross for God's church couldn't be all bad.

Wednesday afternoon was slow, and for once she was able to get out on time. Kim felt a sense of trepidation as she drove to Wyatt's. Should she apologize? No doubt Wyatt didn't appreciate a stranger meddling in his business. Would he treat her as coldly tonight as he had that night?

She found herself thinking about him too much for her own comfort. Her inability to choose the right man had caused her numerous heartbreaks in the past. Her attraction to bad boys always resulted in her being the one who was hurt.

Kim found it embarrassing that the girlfriends she'd grown up with had married and had children while she kept messing up. She'd become rather adept at avoiding her matchmaking friends' attempts to set her up.

She hated to think her self-imposed title of drama queen ran over into her love life, but it did. Every relationship ended with major drama. She'd read the self-help books. She didn't consciously look for men her parents wouldn't approve of. She loved and respected them enough that she'd never do that. Nor was it a latent desire to show her wicked side by choosing men with charming, self-confident personalities who were totally unreliable.

Kim prayed for the right man but second-guessed herself, convinced she needed to show God's love to these men. And after the relationships ended she fantasized about the could-have-beens. A friend had once told Kim her need to save the world spilled over into her relationships. Kim couldn't dispute that.

The last one had been the worst ever. He'd ended up in jail after using money he'd borrowed from her to scam a number of senior citizens, including a couple she'd introduced to him at the store. He'd had the nerve to write her, claiming it wasn't his fault. Just how gullible did he think she was?

She'd gone to talk with Pastor Joe, and he'd told her she would never be happy as long as the men didn't share her faith and similar moral views and outlooks on other matters that were important to her. That was the moment she vowed to God she would never choose another bad boy.

Maybe it was her love for Beth and Chase that made her want Wyatt Alexander to be different for them. Or maybe she feared he was the kind of man she could be attracted to. Whatever the case, she had a promise to keep.

Because of her tight schedule, Kim called in an order for pizza at her favorite place and picked it up on her way out. Maybe she could interest Wyatt in joining her for dinner. She parked in the space in front of his building, and his dog came running. Kim lifted the box higher to keep it from the dog and jumped when he threw back his head and howled. She hurried to the front door.

Wyatt had taped a note there telling her to come around to the side entrance. Kim followed the narrow walkway toward the sound of pounding. She stepped inside then stopped at the sight of Wyatt beating the cross with a chain. "What are you doing?"

He glanced up at her. "Giving it character. You wanted an old rugged cross."

She could see the dents in the wood and the way he'd chopped rather than sawed the ends. He'd even used rope to lash the poles together. Wyatt stood the cross up on the footing he'd created.

"Is that safe to stand on?"

When he nodded, she stepped onto the platform and rested against the cross. "Chase hits me about here. What do you think? Tall enough?"

"Chase?"

She noted Wyatt's pallor. "Yes, he's playing Jesus and doing a wonderful job."

He didn't say anything, and Kim figured she'd better change the subject. She stepped down from the platform, catching Wyatt's hand when it seemed a bit far to the concrete floor. She hoped Chase was more flexible. If not, she'd make another step for him.

Kim walked over to where she'd left the pizza box on his workbench. "You like pizza with the works?"

He joined her. "Sure."

She handed him a couple of napkins and held out the box. Wyatt picked up a slice of pizza and took a big bite. Kim paused to say grace before taking her first bite.

Since she saw no place to sit, she leaned against the workbench and ate her pizza. "I'm thinking of remodeling my kitchen. What do you think? Store-bought or custom-built cabinets?"

Wyatt frowned. "You really need to ask?"

She grinned. "I suppose not. Would you care to give me an estimate?"

"I don't need work. I have more than enough."

"I really need new cabinets. Mine are literally falling apart. The front came off my silverware drawer last night."

"I could fix that for you."

"I already tried wood glue and duct tape. I want a new kitchen with dark cherry wood cabinets, black granite countertops, and stainless steel appliances."

He looked impressed. "You've done some planning."

"Mostly dreaming," Kim said, lifting the pizza box and offering it to him. "Eat all you want. I never eat more than a couple of slices. I want one of those revolving cabinets and a pantry. Maybe some drawers for pots. And drawers deep enough that stuff won't get stuck when I try to open them."

Wyatt half smiled at her comment. "That has more to do with the contents than the depth. There's no such thing as a bottomless drawer."

"True."

"You don't want to jump into this right now," he warned. "Renovation isn't the easiest experience at the best of times."

He had a point. She didn't need to be required to make any more decisions. "Maybe in April after the play is over?"

Wyatt wiped his hands on the napkin before going out front to the desk. Kim could see him through the open door and watched him dig around a few minutes before he came back with a kitchen-planning guide. "Use this to choose the cabinet designs. I can take the measurements later if you still want to do the remodel."

"Oh, I want to do this," Kim said confidently. "Once I make up my mind, there's no going back."

His dark eyebrows shot upward. "That can't make life easy for you."

"I believe people should stand by their commitments."

"When there's a commitment," Wyatt agreed. "In this case you expressed a desire to redo your kitchen, and I'm taking that to mean you want an estimate. There's no commitment until you sign a contract. Unless you're trying to make a point about something else?"

"No," Kim assured him quickly. "I can understand why you might think that. I owe you an apology for the other night. Mrs. Allene's situation had me upset, and I took it out on you. Your personal life is none of my concern."

"People often have reasons for their actions," Wyatt said. "You should never judge anyone until you know all the facts. And you can't possibly know the situation in my family."

Kim felt thoroughly chastened. "I can only promise to try to keep my nose out of your business. I love Beth and Chase a great deal. Their happiness is important to me. I hope you can accept that."

"No, I can't. Until a few days ago you were in the dark about my existence, and now you're feeling enlightened. Beth and I have an agreement, and you can rest assured my son lacks nothing."

"Just his father." The words popped out before she could stop them. "I'm sorry. I shouldn't have said that."

"No, you shouldn't have," Wyatt agreed. "I have to get back to work. Are you okay with the cross?"

"It's exactly what I wanted."

"I'll bring it over to the church when it's done. I need to stain it first."

"We can take care of that," Kim said.

"Thanks, but no. Every piece that comes from Alexander Woodworking is as detailed and precise as I can make it. I believe in doing the right thing when it comes to business."

Kim got the point. Score one for Wyatt. "I'll leave you to your work. Again, thanks for your efforts on behalf of Cornerstone."

"No problem." Wyatt turned back to his work.

Her appetite had disappeared. Feeling dismissed, Kim said, "I'll leave the pizza."

"Thanks for dinner."

She went out the side door. That hadn't gone well. Granted, she'd involved herself in something that was none of her business, but she'd done it out of love for her fellow man. She wasn't judging him. Was she? Maybe it did come across that way.

seven

January slipped into February, and Kim was happy with most aspects of their progress. While everything else was right on schedule, the children were proving to be the problem. Tonight was no different.

She had stressed to the main characters the importance of showing up for practice, but many nights she reassigned roles to another child with the proviso that the role belonged to the original child when he or she came back.

Most of the children wanted to be in the play so badly they were okay with the stand-in roles. Kim found herself reworking the script to add roles for the more dedicated children.

Mari pulled out a chair and sat down beside her. "I'm sure Jesus is pleased to see we have five new disciples tonight."

Kim nodded. "I have a vision of every child who has ever visited Cornerstone, showing up the night of the play and my having to explain to their parents why they can't perform. I don't care, though. I'll fill every role regardless of whether I have to use boys or girls."

Mari smiled at Kim's determination. "And we're working on getting them dressed. You should see some of the costumes. Natalie glued feathers on her wings."

Kim glanced at her. "Really?"

Mari nodded. "We have some fancy costumes, including a crown for the king. One of the senior ladies made it from a piece of gold fabric and glued on the stones."

Their dedication touched Kim. "This is so incredible. I expected simple stuff. The children will be thrilled."

Mari nodded. "We know a shot of confidence can come from feeling well dressed."

Kim smiled at her. "We'd better get this practice underway." She stood and called, "Jesus is coming! Where is my crowd?"

Jesus walked into the room, surrounded by children shouting, "Jesus is coming!"

"Are you sure about Bryan?" Mari asked when the boy slipped in the side door.

"Playing Peter? There's something right about that, don't you think? I know he can be mischievous."

Mari flashed Kim a wide-eyed look of amazement.

"Okay," she admitted. "He's a major brat, but he can handle the role. Maybe it's not smart, but I felt led of God to do it."

"Did God lead you to pair Natalie and Avery on those stones?"

"Exactly," Kim said with a huge grin. "Think of the greater good. Avery needs to stop viewing Natalie as a competitor and start seeing her as a sister in Christ."

"And you're hoping he'll see this through working together with her for the church's greater good?"

"It's doubtful. Natalie's already referring to Avery as a control freak."

"That's not surprising," Mari murmured with a little laugh.

"You think I should separate them?"

"Of course not. We teach the children to love one another. This is Avery's and Natalie's opportunity to show Christian love for each other."

"Let's hope it works. Good thing those stones are made of papier-mâché."

Mari giggled. "Oh, Julie called today. She sold her condo and will be here next week."

"I'm sure Noah's happy about that."

"Ecstatic. He's missed her so much."

"Did they find a place yet? I heard a two-bedroom unit in my building is coming open soon."

"You might want to mention it to Noah. He's been looking but refuses to finalize anything until Julie gets here. I can't say I blame him. Joe got the parsonage, so it wasn't a question of where we wanted to live, but if I'd had to choose I'd have wanted something bigger and newer."

"Some churches give their pastors a housing allowance. I think it's a good idea. At least that way they have an investment for the future."

A cry alerted them to mischief. Kim looked at Mari before she walked over to where Bryan had shoved another child. "What's going on here?"

The boy looked so sweet sugar wouldn't melt in his mouth, and the smaller child looked frightened. Kim took Bryan's arm and walked with him into an empty classroom. "Why are you bullying the smaller children?"

Bryan looked down at his feet. Kim lifted his chin and looked directly into his eyes. "What does God think of bullies?"

"He doesn't like them," the boy mumbled.

"Then why would you do it, Bryan?"

"He gave Jeremy a sucker but wouldn't share with me."

"Are you going to abuse everyone who doesn't share with you?"

"No, ma'am."

"Good. I want you in the play, but I can't allow you to mistreat the other children. Do you understand?"

He nodded, and Kim patted his shoulder. Here again her attraction to bad boys had come through. She could see something in Bryan that few others saw. He could do this. She knew he could. "How are your lines coming along?"

The child perked up. "I know them. Wanna hear?"

"I will as we go through the play. I think you owe Enrique an apology."

She escorted him back to the fellowship hall and waited for him to say he was sorry before leaving him with the other children.

Back in the fellowship hall she noticed the cross standing near the door. Her gaze shifted around the room until she saw Wyatt sitting along the sidelines. He half smiled and lifted his hand in greeting.

On stage Chase spoke his lines, and Wyatt's gaze moved to the boy.

Kim walked over to where he sat. "He's good, don't you think?"

"He appears to know what he's doing."

"Wish I could say the same for all of them," Kim commented as the narrator prompted the kids who forgot their lines in the Lord's Supper scene.

She groaned and covered her face. "This is the easiest line in the play, and they can't get it out."

He looked doubtful. "Why are you doing this?"

"To share the message."

"Isn't that the pastor's job?"

"Pastor Joe does an excellent job, but he needs help," Kim said.

"Seems like a lot of work for a program that lasts an hour or so."

Kim shrugged. "The choir practices every week for months before performing the cantata."

"Are they doing that for Easter?"

"Yes. The choir will perform on Palm Sunday night. Our play is on Good Friday night."

"Well, I brought your cross. I made an adjustment on the step height."

"You didn't have to do that," Kim said.

"It didn't take long. You want it on the stage?"

"Can you wait a few minutes?"

He nodded, and Kim rose from the chair as the children missed their marks again. "Time to direct."

&

Wyatt relaxed in the chair and glanced about the room. This was the first time he'd been near the church of his childhood in years. Nothing much had changed beyond the carpet and pew cushions. His parents had insisted he and Beth attend church. He hadn't minded so much when he was younger, but when he became a teen Wyatt resented being forced.

None of his friends went to Cornerstone, and he'd been stuck with lots of kids he didn't like. Of course, he hadn't gone out of his way to make himself popular either. He'd tolerated the situation for years, even after he and Karen were married. But after Karen's death he decided he was an adult and would do what he wanted.

His decision caused a rift between him and his father. Wilbur Alexander had very little tolerance for a son who refused to serve God. Wyatt wanted his father to accept his right to decide what he wanted to do with his life, but they still had their differences over the situation.

Occasionally Beth argued that his past was old news and it wasn't the same church he remembered, but Wyatt had trouble believing that.

Strangely enough he didn't feel the same level of discomfort tonight. Could it be because Kim made him feel welcome?

When the time for the cross came, Wyatt carried it up onto the stage area.

"That's perfect," Kim told him. "Now we need a stage to raise the children six or eight inches so the audience can see them better."

What did it take? Some measurements, lumber, nails, or screws. What made that so impossible?

"We have plenty of donated lumber but no carpenters," Kim explained.

He could walk away, too, but when Wyatt looked into Kim's eyes he knew he couldn't say no. He found it very difficult to refuse her anything. "I can build one."

"Oh, that would be wonderful!" Kim exclaimed. "I so want them to be seen."

He couldn't help but wonder why her happiness gave him such great satisfaction.

The play demanded her attention again, and he sat down to watch. After practice was over and most of the kids had left with their parents, Wyatt asked Kim if she'd eaten.

"I came over here right after work to get prepared."

"How about joining me?"

She hesitated.

"We need to discuss the plans for the stage," he added. He wasn't playing fair, but he didn't necessarily feel she'd been playing fair when she mentioned the stage in the first place. He suspected Kim recognized him as a soft touch. Oddly enough he'd always been harder than nails for everyone else.

"What restaurant did you have in mind?"

"One that serves steak and potatoes?" At her dismayed look he grinned. "Nothing that heavy, I promise. I'd never sleep tonight."

"Me either. Perhaps a place that serves soup or salad with sandwiches?"

"You want to ride together or drive your car? I can bring you back here."

"I'll ride with you."

Mari came over with the boys to say good night.

"Mari Dennis, this is Wyatt Alexander. He built our cross." She looked at him and said, "Mari is our pastor's wife. These are her three oldest sons, Matthew, Mark, and Luke."

Mari reached to shake his hand. "The cross is spectacular."

"Nice to meet you, Mrs. Dennis," Wyatt said. "You, too, guys. As for the cross, Kim gives good instructions."

"I can't take credit," Kim denied quickly. "It's so much nicer than anything I imagined."

"I try."

"We're out of here," Mari said, grabbing the youngest boy's shoulders and guiding him toward the door. "See you Sunday, Kim. We'd love to see you, too, Mr. Alexander."

After the lights had been turned out and the church locked up, Kim settled in Wyatt's truck. They discussed restaurants and agreed on a place that met both their needs.

After ordering their food they sipped iced tea, and Wyatt used her pen to sketch out on a scrap of paper a plan for the stage.

"Just let me know when you want to get the measurements."

"What's the earliest we can clear the area?" he asked.

"Thursday morning, I suppose."

"The stage will need to be broken down afterward?"

"We'll have Saturday to put everything back together. Do you plan to build the stage in place or move it there later? I can ask Pastor Joe for volunteers to assist you."

"Get the volunteers, and we'll decide. If we don't have sufficient manpower, I can build it in place."

Their food arrived, and Kim concentrated on the broccoli and cheese soup she'd chosen. "This is delicious."

Wyatt took a bite of his burger. "I was hungrier than I realized."

Kim remembered the plans in her purse. She swallowed hastily, coughing when the soup went down the wrong way.

"Are you okay? Here," he said, lifting her glass from the table. "Take a sip of tea."

Kim coughed and spluttered for a moment longer, then said, "I'm okay. I wanted to show you my kitchen plans." She grabbed her oversized satchel and dug around until she located the planning sheet he'd given her.

"You won't need a kitchen if you choke to death."

She laughed and unfolded the pages. She smoothed them out and placed them in the center of the table, facing him. "What do you think?"

He picked up the sheet. "Looks like you've figured out what you want."

"I'm excited about redoing the kitchen," Kim said. "That planning guide made the choices so much easier."

"But you agree you need to wait until after the program to start work?"

Kim sighed. "Yes. Will you put me on your calendar for April?"

"I'll see what's pending. We can do some of the preliminary planning to help move the plans along. And I'm getting a new saw with a built-in computer."

"How does that work?" Kim spooned more soup into her mouth.

"You put specific measurements into the computer, and it directs the cutting of the boards. I figure it will pay for itself. Even experienced carpenters make mistakes."

"But not often," Kim countered.

Wyatt wiped his mouth. "Not if we can help ourselves. It cuts into the profit margin."

"How did you get into carpentry work?"

"I was hooked when I took a class in high school. Dad had the equipment sitting in his shop, and once I learned how to use it I wanted to build stuff all the time. It became an expensive hobby."

"So you turned it into a way to make a living?"

Wyatt dropped his napkin on the table and pushed his plate away. "Not at first. Dad works for a soda distributor, and he got me a delivery job. Karen and I had just married, and he insisted I needed something dependable. It's logical he'd feel that way. He's worked for the company for more than thirty years.

"Anyway, I went to work for them and did woodwork on my own time. Soon everyone in the family had more wooden bowls than they needed."

"You made Beth's fruit bowl, didn't you?" Kim asked. When he nodded, she said, "It's gorgeous. You should sell them. I'd buy one."

He chuckled. "I'll keep that in mind."

"So when did you start your company?"

"About three years ago. The distributing company required a clean driving record, so the accident and subsequent driving-under-the-influence charge put me out of work. Dad was furious. Not because I caused my wife's death but because I'd lost my job."

"You made a bad choice, Wyatt. I think you should forgive yourself."

"I wish I could. It makes me sick every time I think about how I deprived Chase of his mother. I don't deserve his love."

"So you think your guilt is sufficient reason to deprive him of both parents?"

"You don't understand."

"Maybe I don't," Kim agreed. "Let's don't argue. Tell me about the business."

"I got a job with a cabinetmaker and spent the next few years learning the trade. About three years ago the owner decided to retire and offered me his equipment at a good price. I got a loan, and Alexander Woodworking was born. I put up that metal building behind the house and started work. I haven't looked back since."

"You work alone?"

"I have a couple of part-time people who help out. They're retired and like a few hours now and then. The cabinets pay the bills, but the specialty pieces are my favorites. My house is full of furniture I built."

"I'd love to see it."

"Anytime," he told her. The waiter asked if he wanted more tea, and Wyatt shook his head. "It's late. Guess we'd better let these people go home."

He took care of the bill and escorted her to his truck. "Maybe next time you can tell me about you," he said as he fastened his seatbelt and started the vehicle.

"I don't consider myself anywhere near as interesting."

He looked at her, and their gazes caught. "Let me decide for myself."

"Only if you agree I can do the same."

He leaned closer and kissed her softly.

Kim pulled back. "Wyatt. . . I . . . we. . . why did you do that?"

"I wanted to."

Kim didn't know how to respond.

eight

Kim found her thoughts returning to Wyatt and the kiss more often than she liked. The feeling that he didn't give himself as much credit as he should remained foremost in her mind, though.

The accident that killed his wife had started a downhill spiral that had only become worse over the years. He'd suffered and grieved alone, staying away from Chase and his family because he didn't feel he deserved to be loved.

If only he realized God loved him despite his poor choices and welcomed the opportunity to share that love with him. Kim knew that except for that very same grace she would be in the same place as Wyatt.

The realization that she was more attracted to him than she should be struck Kim. She knew she was in danger of breaking the promise she'd made to God. She couldn't become involved with Wyatt Alexander. He wasn't a Christian. They didn't share the same faith. She would end up getting her heart broken.

As if worrying about Wyatt wasn't enough, Kim found each passing week brought a fresh feeling of panic. The issue of the kids' attendance still hadn't been resolved, and most of them needed a great deal of work on their lines. They had a couple of weeks before they needed to pick up the pace, and she hoped they could settle everything before the night of the play.

Julie arrived on Monday, and Maggie, Mari, and Kim decided to celebrate by doing lunch and some shopping on Saturday.

"Welcome to the beach," Kim said as she hugged Julie.

Kim had told Noah about the unit in her building, and the couple had taken a look. Julie liked the setup, especially the closeness to the beach, and it appeared Kim might soon have even more Cornerstone neighbors.

When they discussed restaurants, Kim mentioned the place she and Wyatt had visited. "They have excellent soup and salads. Wyatt said the burgers were good, too."

Mari glanced at her with raised brows. "That sounds suspiciously like a date."

"We were discussing plans for the stage at church. I took pizza over to his shop when I went to look at the cross, and I'm sure he felt the need to return the favor."

"You're not getting in over your head, are you?" Maggie asked.

When she didn't speak, Julie looked around the group. "Anyone care to fill me in on what's going on?"

"Do you want to tell her, Kim?" Maggie asked.

She shrugged. "If Julie's going to be one of my friends, she needs to know what a lousy judge of men I am."

"It's not your fault you have bad luck with relationships," Maggie said.

"Oh, come on," Kim said. "I make the choices. I'm a bad-boy magnet," she told Julie. "If there's a man out there destined to break a woman's heart, he comes at me like a heat-seeking missile."

"And you keep making the same mistake over and over?" Julie guessed. When Kim nodded, she said, "I suspect women typically choose the same type of men. It all has to do with traits that appeal to us. It's not an outward appearance thing either."

"So how do I lose this fascination for the wrong type of man? I promised I wouldn't become involved with another man who would break my heart, but I find myself thinking

Wyatt Alexander doesn't give himself the credit he deserves."

"He's not a Christian," Mari reminded her. "That's your first warning. You can't hope to understand each other's needs if you're not on the same level spiritually."

"I know, but he's hurting," Kim said, sadness weighing heavily on her heart. "I'm certain his unhappiness stems from one bad decision he made years ago."

"You can't save him, Kim," Maggie said. "Leave that in God's more than capable hands. When He's ready for you to meet the right man, you'll be the first to know."

"Maggie's right about that," Julie offered. "I had some serious anger issues with Noah. I'd made up my mind we'd never work things out, but God interceded on my behalf—and look where we are now."

"God helped you improve your relationship with Him. Once that happened, you were able to have a loving relationship with Noah," Mari pointed out.

"I know Wyatt has to be the one to change his life, but he needs guidance."

"Not yours, Kim," Mari warned. "You're already borderline fascinated with the man. First thing you know, you'll be in love and heading for heartbreak."

"He kissed me."

"What did you say?" Maggie asked, her eyes wide.

"I was in shock, too. I asked why he did it, and he said he wanted to."

"What are you going to do?" Mari asked.

"I don't know. I've got too much on my plate right now to worry about relationships. I'm about ready to pull my hair out with this group of children. I've yet to get the disciples to say that one line right."

They discussed the play for a few minutes before the conversation eased into other topics. Kim took a sip of soft drink and set her glass on the table. "How is Mrs. Allene?"

"Not good. The chemo makes her nauseous."

"They've brought medicine so far, you'd think they could figure out how to keep it from making the patients so sick."

"I'm praying things will improve. It's heartbreaking to see her suffer so."

"Did she call her son?"

Maggie frowned slightly as she shook her head. "I'm staying out of it. I'll do what I can for Mrs. Allene. She's my friend, and I love her a great deal."

"I'm sure she'll call him soon," Kim said.

"Do you think Joey should contact him?" Julie asked.

The other three women looked at each other and shook their heads in unison.

"We've already asked, and Joe believes it is Mrs. Allene's decision," Mari said. "He says she'll call her son when she's ready."

"Wyatt says the same thing," Kim offered.

All three heads turned in her direction, and she held up her hands. "We talked that night after Maggie and I tried to convince Mrs. Allene to make the call. I thought he'd agree with us, but his advice was to stay out of her business."

"I don't get it," Julie said. "Our parents died so suddenly. I can't imagine that Joey would want anyone to give up an opportunity to spend time with their loved ones."

"Joe can't allow his personal feelings to come before Mrs. Allene's wishes," Mari said.

"Maybe it's a man-woman thing," Julie said.

"I'm surprised you told Wyatt," Maggie said.

"He remembered Mrs. Allene from his childhood Sunday school years."

"I'm finding myself more and more intrigued about this Wyatt guy," Julie admitted.

"He's cute," Mari told her. "I met him at play practice."

"I'm sure you'll see him around the church a time or two

before the play. I'm hoping he'll attend the play as well."

"Who knows? You might be more of a draw than you realize," Julie said.

A couple of days later Wyatt called about getting measurements for the stage. They arranged to meet at the church around two, but she had to cancel.

She dialed his number. "Wyatt? It's Kim. I'm tied up here at the store. My salesclerk Ruby had to pick up her sick child at daycare. Pastor Joe says to come by the church office. He knows exactly what we want so it shouldn't be any problem. I'm truly sorry."

"Did you want me to come by later to get those kitchen measurements?"

"Call me after you finish at the church, and I should be able to let you know if we can make it work."

༄

That afternoon Wyatt parked by the church office and went inside. The secretary immediately called the pastor. He came out of his office and reached to shake Wyatt's hand. "Good to see you, Mr. Alexander."

"Call me Wyatt."

"Only if you'll call me Joe."

Wyatt wasn't exactly comfortable with that. "What if I call you Pastor Joe?"

"That'll do."

The two men worked together pulling measurements and discussing what needed to be done to make the stage work.

"Noah and I will help. Do you think you'll need more men?"

"I can probably get my helpers if we need them," Wyatt said, amazed that he'd just offered to provide laborers for a volunteer job. Oh, well, it wouldn't hurt him to spend a few bucks for a good cause. Particularly since his son played such a key role in the performance.

"I'm sure Kim's told you how appreciative we are of your help."

He slipped the notepad and pencil into his pocket. "She has."

"I hear Beth says you're the best carpenter she knows."

Wyatt felt slightly embarrassed. "Definitely a kid-sister kind of statement, don't you think?"

Pastor Joe nodded. "My sister tells everyone I'm the best pastor she knows. It's going to cause her problems now that she's married to a pastor. I suppose I'll get demoted to second best."

The two men laughed and walked over to sit on the front pew.

"Why haven't I seen you here before?" Pastor Joe asked.

"I haven't attended Cornerstone since my wife was killed."

"Why?"

Wyatt didn't find himself uncomfortable with the pastor's question. "You know my parents." Pastor Joe acknowledged he did. "Well, their church philosophy was that as long as I lived in their house, they decided where and when I went to church. They weren't above coercion. My desire to participate in team sports or even hang out with my friends gave them means. On Sundays I couldn't leave the house unless I went to church first."

"You resented that?"

Wyatt nodded. "None of my friends attended Cornerstone, and I wanted to be with them. Of course, my friends didn't attend church anywhere. They were like me, sneaking around doing stuff they had no business doing. And every time the church doors opened, I had to show up, more than a little aware that I wasn't deceiving God with my presence."

"Did you feel guilty?"

He shrugged. "Maybe a little at first. Mostly I tuned the messages out and thought about my plans for the afternoon. Things like where we would hang out and who was bringing the beer."

"I think every parent hopes their children will develop a love for God. If they can't reach them, they pray someone else can. I know how I feel about my five children."

"I met three of them," Wyatt said.

Pastor Joe pulled his wallet from his pocket and showed Wyatt the family photo he carried with him. "The two little ones are twenty-month-old twins."

"Nice-looking family."

Pastor Joe nodded his agreement. "Mari is the love of my life. Nothing would be the same without her. I was working as an investment banker when we met. My parents had died, and I'd assumed guardianship of my teenage sister. Mari loved Julie and cared for her like her own sister.

"When I felt led to become a minister, I thought Mari would disagree. At that point we had three boys, Julie had just graduated from college, and I knew financial security would be an issue for Mari. To tell the truth, it was for me, too. I didn't see how I could support my family and do God's work. But He showed me the way.

"Sorry. I turned this onto me, but what I wanted to say was I was one of the fortunate ones. My parents raised us in a Christian home. When they were killed in a car accident, I knew God had His reasons even though they were far beyond my comprehension. I never resented going to church because I'd developed a love relationship with Him."

"A love relationship?"

Pastor Joe nodded. "The Bible says, 'Love the Lord thy God with all thine heart, and with all thy soul, and with all thy might.' People think I love God because I'm a minister, but it's more than that. The relationship goes beyond what I feel for my family or friends. God is first in my life."

"Why do you suppose I never developed that rapport?"

"Could be you resented your parents for controlling your life so much you refused to allow God to do the same."

"I wasn't ready to do God's work, but my parents didn't want to hear that. After high school I met Karen at the club where she worked. She'd come to the beach with the intention of partying for a while before she settled down.

"We hooked up, and when Chase was on the way we married. Her parents lived in Florida, so she didn't have to worry about anyone forcing her to go to church."

"Our Chase?"

Wyatt nodded. "He's my son."

"How did your wife die?"

"In an accident," Wyatt told him. "We were happy, or I suppose we thought we were. Our lives had a comfortable sameness. We'd work all week, and on the weekends we'd get my parents or Beth to babysit so we could party.

"We'd been to a party the night she died. Both of us had more to drink than we should have. A semi in front of us had a blowout. I was following too close and ended up flipping the car."

"It could have happened if you'd been sober."

"Killing Karen was bad enough, but I lost my foot, too. Because of one stupid decision I deprived my son of his mother and stuck him with a crippled father. In fact, that night Chase hadn't felt well. He had a cold, and Karen wasn't sure we should leave him. I convinced her it was okay. If I'd listened, she'd still be alive today."

"You can 'what if' the situation to death, but the truth is that only God knows what the future holds. We make our mistakes when we try to guide God instead of allowing Him to guide us."

"You mean like leaving Chase with my family instead of raising him myself?"

"You made the decision based on the grief and pain you were feeling at the time. You loved your wife and son and believed you couldn't make a difference for her but were determined to make a difference for Chase."

"Beth's been good for him."

"Your sister is a good woman. She loves Chase. And I know she worries about your salvation."

"I wish she wouldn't."

"That's the way of Christians when it comes to the people we love, Wyatt. Praying for you isn't something we turn on and off at will. God lays a burden on our hearts for every lost lamb, regardless of whether you're our own flesh and blood or a stranger. When we take on the mantle of Christ, we become His disciples." He paused for a moment, reflected, then asked, "Wyatt, are you angry at God?"

Wyatt shook his head. "No. I just feel He has no need for an old sinner like me."

"Did you ever accept Him as your personal Savior?"

"I made a declaration and carried through with baptism at fourteen, even though I wasn't sincere. I did it to fool my parents and everyone else."

"But you didn't fool God."

"No. I was two-faced. One for the people at church, another for my friends. Neither group knew the other existed."

"What are you feeling now, Wyatt?"

"Honestly, I don't know. When Kim asked me to build a cross, I couldn't believe I agreed to do it. Then when she mentioned this stage I offered again. Believe me when I say I don't usually do anything for the church."

"Perhaps God has presented you with the opportunity of service. I'm sure He appreciates the way you've responded. Cornerstone has another project we could use your help with."

"What's that?"

"The church has a large stained-glass window scheduled to arrive two weeks before Easter. We're planning a dedication service for Easter morning. We have to prepare the area for the window. It involves cutting out that wall and framing it up for a fixed window. I've been asking around, and our builders are tied up with construction projects. I'd hate to disappoint the congregation by not getting it in place."

"Let me check my schedule." As soon as he spoke the words, Wyatt wondered what possessed him to keep agreeing to help with Cornerstone's needs. "I'd better get going."

"God loves you, Wyatt. No matter what poor decisions you've made in the past, God has a plan for your future. He wants to bless you."

"Thanks, Pastor Joe. Maybe if we'd had a minister like you here at Cornerstone when I was growing up, I'd have that love relationship you speak of."

"Can we pray before you go?"

The pastor rested his hand on Wyatt's shoulder. "Our precious heavenly Father, we come to You, seeking understanding. We praise You for sending Wyatt to Cornerstone to help in Your work. Please guide his hands in the building of these projects, and may they be used to glorify You in the production of the Easter play.

"Lord, Wyatt has other needs. He's feeling regret because of past experiences. Help him understand that, no matter what he's done, You died for him. Help him accept that forgiveness and grow in his love for You. And help him realize the ways of the world are not Your ways and be with him as he begins his walk with You."

"You sound like it's a given I'll find Jesus," Wyatt said.

"I feel you already have. My question is, what are you going to do next?"

Wyatt stood. "I'd better go."

"Nice meeting you, Wyatt. I'm here at the church anytime you feel like talking."

"Thanks."

Back in his truck Wyatt reached for his cell phone and

dialed Kim's number. "I'm just leaving the church. Can we meet another night?"

"Sure. Is everything okay?"

"Yeah. Fine. I met with Pastor Joe and got the measurements for the stage. It shouldn't be a problem."

"I'm glad he was able to help."

"He's a nice guy."

"The church has been blessed by his presence. You should hear him preach. He and Noah Loughlin are truly men of God."

"I'll follow up on those measurements soon."

"Sure. Take care."

Wyatt picked up a burger at a drive-thru and headed straight for his workshop.

His conversation with Joe Dennis played heavily on his mind. Particularly that statement about him finding Jesus. Pastor Joe struck him as very different from the ministers of his past. He felt tempted to attend one of the man's sermons. Somehow he doubted this man's spin on fire and brimstone would be similar to the sermons of his youth. Those pastors had convinced him he'd never make it to heaven.

All these years he'd resented his father and avoided God, but since that first day Kimberly Elliott set foot in his shop he'd agreed not only to one project but now three. Even though he hadn't said yes to the Good Shepherd window, Wyatt had no doubt he would help.

But the real question for him was, why was he doing all this? Why was he agreeing to job after job for the church? Was Joe Dennis right? Was God directing his path?

Maybe it was time. He hadn't done such a great job on his own. He'd been impressed by more than Joe's personality. The pastor exhibited the sense of peace Wyatt had craved his entire life.

When he'd partied he had sought answers in beer, loud

music, and other people, but he'd never found them. After he lost Karen he kept to himself and concentrated on making his business successful. In his rare spare time, he hunted and fished and tried not to think about the pain of his losses.

Not a day went by that he didn't miss his son. He felt a stabbing pain in his heart every time he saw Chase with Beth. He'd avoided family get-togethers for that very reason. He knew his son was getting older and didn't understand why his father wanted nothing to do with him.

It wasn't that he didn't want his son—he just didn't want to confuse the boy any more than he already had. For ten years he'd turned over his parental rights to Beth. Was it fair to Chase to step back into his life now?

Joe Dennis had given him so much to think about today.

And even some things to pray about.

nine

As the days flew past, Kim felt the growing pressure to see things finalized. The groundhog's prediction of another six weeks of cold weather made part of her look forward to spring while another part told her spring would bring the play.

Wyatt had come over to get the measurements for the kitchen, and Kim sensed a change in him. He seemed happier. She wondered why. Maybe he'd taken on a big project for his business.

She'd expected to be uncomfortable around him, but he kept things all business.

He'd wowed her with a wooden bowl. "I think this is the color you wanted?"

Kim found the dark cherrywood absolutely perfect. "This is fantastic."

"I'll keep that stain in mind when I finish building the cabinets. I have a stone sample you may want to look at for a backsplash."

It surprised her that Wyatt had used his own time to find materials for her kitchen. "Sure. I'm debating. The glass tiles are gorgeous."

"Costly. What about stainless steel?"

"Cold. Tile can be cold, too, but I like it better. I want designer tiles."

"Did you look at the granite?"

"Mari and I rode over there a couple of weeks ago. I found one I really liked. The owner said he was pretty sure it would work with cherry cabinets. I'd appreciate your opinion if you have time."

"I need to go over there in a couple of days. I'll take a look. Have you considered flooring?"

"I don't have any idea what I want. I'd thought about wood, bamboo even, but I'm afraid I'll have too much wood."

"Is there such a thing as too much wood?" Wyatt teased, joining in when she burst into laughter.

"Wood, stone, and tile will definitely need something to soften it."

"Have you considered a kitchen designer?"

"I visited a couple of showrooms and noted things I liked. I'm going to get tile and floor contractors to do the work, but I need to coordinate everything to keep costs down. My budget won't stretch as far if I hire a consultant to do the work."

"Some companies offer the service free when you buy their products."

"But I'm not buying their product. You don't offer design services, do you?"

Wyatt shook his head. "I'm strictly a cabinetmaker."

"And I'm taking your advice and not worrying about this right now."

"Good idea."

"Pastor Joe told me you've agreed to help with the Good Shepherd window."

Wyatt nodded. "He mentioned it the day I went for the stage measurements. He called me a couple of days later, and I said yes."

"I can't wait to see it in place," Kim exclaimed.

"I haven't seen the window, but Pastor Joe assures me it's a beautiful stained-glass piece."

"Mari said he's very impressed with you."

"I'm not impressive."

"Cut yourself some slack, Wyatt. Pastor Joe is a good judge of character."

"I'm definitely a character."

"I'd say you're hopeless, but you'd agree with me."

He nodded. "I would."

❧

The drama committee had scheduled a work night for the last Tuesday in February. Kim was eager to know where they stood in terms of costumes and props.

She drove over to the church to find people already at work. Mari worked with the women who had agreed to sew costumes. Two women cut out the garments while several others used portable machines on the long tables.

They chattered as they worked, quickly sewing together the sides of the garments before they hemmed the neck, sleeves, and bottoms. Other women pressed the pieces and placed them on hangers.

She walked over to where Mari had just hung another costume on the rack. "This looks like a production line."

"No one wanted to be left out. I figured the more the merrier."

Kim sorted through the costumes, finding robes with long vests in stripes and fabrics in keeping with the time Jesus and the disciples walked the earth.

"There's a room in back where we can lock away the costumes and props."

"Do we have enough fabric?"

"More than enough," Mari said. She indicated the clothes on the rack. "Most of the ladies who sewed those costumes paid for the material themselves."

"The program is thick with all these acknowledgments."

"Probably best to thank the entire congregation for their support and encouragement and leave it there. You don't want to take a chance on missing anyone."

"Good idea," Kim said.

Mari smiled. "Did you find parts for those other children?"

Kim nodded. "I think so. Where's Maggie?"

"Mrs. Allene took a turn for the worse this afternoon, and they admitted her to the hospital. Maggie said she called her son this weekend. She doesn't think Mrs. Allene told him how bad things are, though, since he only promised to come for a visit soon."

"I'd be furious if my parents did something like this to me," Kim declared.

"I'm sure your parents have their secrets, Kim."

"Did Natalie and Avery show up yet?"

Mari tilted her head to the opposite end of the room. "Avery's over there with his chicken wire and papier-mâché."

Kim glanced over to where Avery Baker worked, noting the black plastic garbage bag he wore to protect his clothing. "You think he'll get Natalie to wear one of those?"

"I seriously doubt it." One of the women called Mari over.

"Go ahead," Kim told her. "I'll grab a bite to eat and find a project."

They had agreed to a potluck, and Kim had gone in with Mari and Maggie to purchase a deli tray and some breads.

Kim smiled at Pastor Joe as she approached the food table. "Good turnout, don't you think?"

"Excellent," he agreed. "People like to be involved."

She slathered a bun with mustard before adding ham, lettuce, and tomato. She spooned potato and pasta salads onto her plate and scooped a serving of homemade banana pudding into a dessert bowl.

"Take this for me," Pastor Joe said, handing her his plate. "I'll get us something to drink."

She chose one of the tables along the side. Pastor Joe placed two cups of tea on the table and sat down. He said grace, and they started to eat. "Heard from Wyatt lately?"

Startled, Kim looked up. "We talked right after you told me he agreed to help with the window. He came over to measure my kitchen."

"You're not getting in over your head, are you?"

She could play dumb, but he'd see right through that. She'd discussed her last breakup with him when she promised before God not to fall into the same trap again.

Pastor Joe had warned her about the importance of carrying through on vows made to God, quoting Ecclesiastes 5:5.

She'd been emphatic that nothing would stand in the way of her achieving her goal to avoid bad boys. "I'm struggling," she admitted. "Every time I'm around Wyatt I see glimpses of a good, decent man, but then I remind myself he's not a Christian."

"And if he were?"

"I probably wouldn't be attracted to him," Kim said.

Pastor Joe's hoot of laughter drew some gazes in their direction. "You're something else, Kimberly Elliott."

"Seriously though, I see Wyatt as his own worst enemy. He's shared some stuff with me, mistakes he made in his youth that have colored his attitude toward life."

Pastor Joe nodded. "I agree. I suspect he shared some of that same history when we talked. But I sensed something happening with him. A change he finds surprising. He can't believe he keeps agreeing to help with these church projects."

Kim giggled. "No doubt he regrets the day he agreed to build the cross for me."

"I don't think so. Do you think he would have given such attention to detail if he didn't care?"

"His carpentry work is important to him. I don't think anything would come out of Wyatt's shop that isn't topnotch. That's the way he works."

"I wouldn't discourage you from friendship with Wyatt, Kim, but look out for yourself. Find a God-fearing decent man and settle into a happy life. That's what God wants for you."

"I know. Believe me, there's nothing I want more than

a man who loves God first, then me, and wants a family. And yet I continually sabotage myself. Why do I find lying cheaters so attractive?"

"That's a question you have to answer for yourself. Is it an attraction to the man himself or the belief that your love can make him a decent human being?" He held up his hand when she started to respond. "Don't answer that for me, Kim. Answer it truthfully for yourself."

"I already know the answer. They see the weakness in me. I lay my heart out there on a platter and take whatever they offer. I dare to believe they have a grain of goodness in them, and maybe for a moment or two they allow the good to shine through; but they always revert to their old ways.

"In their minds it's fair as long as they don't get caught. They figure what I don't know can't hurt me. They never think about the fact that every lie comes to light eventually."

"That's not the life your heavenly Father wants for you."

"Pray for my wayward heart," Kim requested softly.

"That heart is one of my favorite things about you."

"Then pray for God to give me strength, to send the right person to accept the love I need to give. And pray for Wyatt Alexander, that he can accept the love of his heavenly Father and turn his life around. Pray he forgives himself for making the wrong decisions and accepts that the gifts he's already been given are greater than the losses he's incurred."

"I already have. I've prayed for you both. Forgive yourself, too, Kim. Leave those bad decisions you made in those relationships in the past. Concentrate on the future joy God has planned for you."

" 'Delight thyself also in the Lord: and he shall give thee the desires of thine heart,' " Kim quoted.

"Exactly. We'd better finish up here," he added. "I suspect Mari thinks I've wasted enough time eating."

Kim winked at him and began gathering her trash. "I'll tell

her it's my fault. That you were counseling one of your lost sheep."

"She'd never buy that. You're about as lost as the sun in the sky."

"During an eclipse?"

"Things are always darkest before the dawn?" he countered. "Sometime when you have an opportunity I'd like to sit down with you and discuss writing. I have some ideas I'd like to put together, but I don't have a clue how to proceed."

"I'll tell you what I know, but bear in mind that my experience is limited to plays." She looked across the room. "I think I'll see if Natalie and Avery need help with those stones."

"I'll ask Mari what she wants me to do. She'll probably make me iron. She knows I hate ironing." He smiled and turned to go.

"Natalie, Avery," Kim said as she walked over to where they worked. The atmosphere felt so thick she could cut it with a knife. "Looks like these are coming along."

"They would be if Natalie would stop making suggestions," Avery snapped.

"I didn't realize you were a committee of one, Avery. All I said was that we needed to use different shades of gray to cast shadows on the stones."

"Then why don't you let me build them so you can color to your heart's content?"

"Don't be a jerk."

Anger filled his expression.

Kim laid her hands on their backs. "Come on, guys. We're setting an example for the kids here. Can't you put aside your differences for them?"

He glared at Natalie. "It's not my fault. I offered to make the stones, and then she horned in like she always does."

"If you didn't want my help, why didn't you just say so?"

"And have everyone look down on me?" he demanded. "They'd all be saying, 'Poor Natalie. That Avery is such a bad guy.'"

Natalie turned away. "It's useless. I can't work with him, Kim."

"Okay, tell you what. Let's leave Avery with the stones, and we'll build the tomb."

"Hey, I wanted to do that," he objected.

"You can't do everything," Kim told him. "We can all work together as a team, or I'll split the project and we'll work separately. You decide."

"Fine," he said sharply, apparently put out by her mandate. "We can work together."

"I thought so. I'm going to see how everyone else is doing, and then I'll be back. Don't make me separate you two," Kim warned, sounding like a parent chastising her unruly children.

She smiled at Avery's mutterings when he turned on Natalie. "I figured your friend would take your side."

"I can hear you, Avery."

The two of them fascinated her. They'd probably be good friends if Avery could get beyond seeing Natalie as his rival. Of course, Natalie wasn't the type to let Avery browbeat her.

The door opened, and Maggie stepped inside. Kim took a detour over to say hello. "Mari said you were with Mrs. Allene."

"I just left the hospital. They got her settled into a room, and she's sleeping."

"Is it bad?"

Tears clouded Maggie's eyes. "I don't think it will be long. I requested a leave of absence for personal reasons. The hospital agreed."

Kim hugged Maggie close, and they shared their grief at the thought of losing such a good friend. "What about her son?"

"I'm calling him," Maggie declared.

Kim stepped back and looked at her. "Are you sure?"

"Very. I will not let Mrs. Allene go to her grave without the comfort of her only child. I don't care what she says. It's not fair to her or her son. Dillon Rogers needs to be here for his mother."

"Do you have his number?"

"It's on her speed dial. I'm going over there to pack some items, and I'll get it then."

"You need help?"

"I'm good. I can't call myself her friend if I allow her to die alone. I have to do this."

"You don't need to justify the situation for me. I agree that it's the right thing to do."

Maggie looked around the room. "I'm sorry I can't help. Looks like a good turnout."

Kim lowered her voice. "I've been over refereeing Avery and Natalie. I told them I'd separate them if they couldn't play together."

Maggie giggled, and it did Kim's heart good. "Avery is so stubborn. I don't know why Natalie offered to work with him."

"I think she hopes Avery will accept her one day," Maggie said. "She once told me there's more than enough business in this town for both of them."

"But Avery can't stand being second best. He sees Natalie's work and goes off the deep end every time. If she offers something, he has to offer something bigger or better. I believe Natalie is willing to be his friend, but his manly pride refuses to allow that."

"Let's pray the Lord opens his eyes. I asked Pastor Joe to pray for the same for me."

"What's up, Kim?"

"Wyatt Alexander. I'm starting to see his good traits over the bad."

"Don't forget your vow."

"I haven't. It just breaks my heart to see someone so unhappy and not be able to help."

Kim felt the gentle pressure of Maggie's hand against hers. "We can't make other people happy, Kim. They have to do it for themselves. Prayer works. Look what it's done for me."

Maggie hadn't always been a Christian. In fact, she'd come to know the Lord only within the last decade.

"I know," Kim said. "God makes a major difference in all of us when we give Him control. Of course, it's hard to give up that control."

"What exactly do you think you can do for Wyatt Alexander that his family hasn't?"

"Nothing." Kim knew that was true. If they couldn't reach him, what made her think she could? "Let's talk about this later," she suggested. "You need to take care of those things for Mrs. Allene. We can't solve the problem tonight, not even with our best effort."

"I'm praying, Kim."

She hugged Maggie. "Me, too. I'll try to stop by the hospital after work tomorrow to visit Mrs. Allene. Let me know if I can help in any way."

Maggie nodded. "I'm praying for your program, too, Kim. I know it's going to be wonderful."

ten

Wyatt had just come inside to fix himself a sandwich when he heard a tap on the back door and Beth let herself in. "Beth? Where's Chase?"

"At his friend's. We need to talk."

"I just left the shop. You want a sandwich? Something to drink?"

"I'll take a soda."

He pointed to the fridge. "What brings you out here on a school night?"

"Gerald called tonight. He'll be home soon."

"That's great."

"I've missed him." Beth took out a few containers that needed to be thrown away and removed the soda bottle from the back of the shelf. She pulled out a stool and sat down at the island. "I wanted to talk to you about Chase."

"I'm listening." Wyatt took a bite of his sandwich.

"I want Chase to stay with you so Gerald and I can have some time alone."

"Mom would keep him."

His answer seemed to irritate his sister. "Sure she would, but in case you haven't looked lately Mom isn't as young as she used to be. Chase is an active child. He has a number of activities that require someone to drive him back and forth. He needs you, Wyatt."

He laid the sandwich on the paper towel and looked at her. "What is this about, Beth?"

"It's about you being a father to your son."

"Did Kimberly Elliott put you up to this?"

Beth appeared startled. "Why would you think that?"

"It's not the first time my parenting has been mentioned lately."

"I'm sorry, Wyatt, but she's my friend. We did talk the other night after she came here to ask you to build the cross. I wanted her to understand the decision you made."

"I wish you hadn't. She has a tendency to control the situation."

"No, she doesn't. Kim has a tendency to think with her heart rather than her head. If she's said anything to you, it's only because she feels Chase deserves better. That's why I'm here tonight. You know I love him like my own, but I can't help thinking we're not being fair to him."

"Chase is doing fine."

"He's a good kid, but he's nearly a teenager. Don't you remember how confusing those years were?"

"I had both parents and look how I turned out. You honestly think I'm ready to direct Chase's path?"

"It's been ten years, Wyatt. If we wait another ten, he could be married with kids of his own. I'm not joking. The opportunity for you to bond as father and son could be lost. I'm not getting any younger, and neither is Gerald. We're thinking about starting our own family. Kim asked how Chase would feel when that happened. And I honestly don't know."

Wyatt slammed his hand against the countertop. "I knew she had something to do with this."

"And I told you she doesn't."

"So what's this really about?" he asked frostily.

"Gerald is being reassigned to a base in Arizona. He wants us to live together, and I want that, too. So we've reached a decision. If I'm going to be Chase's mother, we'll have to make it legal. Gerald and I will adopt him, and he'll live with us in Arizona and be raised as our son."

The idea hit Wyatt like a kick in the stomach. Although

he hadn't lived with his son since Chase was two, Wyatt had known the comfort of having him just a few minutes away. Could he bear not having him close? "And if I don't agree to adoption?"

"Then you step up to the plate and become the dad Chase deserves."

"You'd trust your heathen brother to raise your precious nephew?"

Beth frowned. "Don't pull that on me, Wyatt. For years I've worried and prayed for you, hoping you'd realize you're not at fault for Karen's death. What if you'd died instead of her? Do you think she would have asked me to raise Chase?"

Wyatt knew his wife would never have considered the idea of someone else parenting their son.

"I love you, and I love Chase," Beth said before he could answer. "I know you love him, too. I see the longing in your eyes when we're all together. Why don't you give him a chance to influence your life for a change? I think you'll be impressed by your son."

The thought scared him. "What if I agree to the adoption?"

"Is that what you want?" Beth asked softly. "To hear him call Gerald Dad? To see Chase once or twice a year? To be totally uninvolved in his life? If we adopt him, we won't accept child support. He'll be our son. Not yours."

He tried to hide his misery from her probing stare. "I want him to be happy, and I'm not sure I'm capable of making that happen. How do you think he's going to feel about being forced to leave the only home he's ever known and come here to live?

"I don't know anything about kids. I work all hours of the day and night. What about getting him to school and those activities you mentioned? Who's going to feed him and make sure his clothes are clean? Make sure he does his homework and gets to bed on time and doesn't watch stuff on television he has no business watching?"

"The brother my parents raised," Beth answered simply as she came to stand beside him, rubbing her hand across his shoulders. "You know how parenting works. You make decisions that may not be popular and live with the consequences. The rest is easy. You cook for yourself. You do laundry. You clean. And Chase does chores at my house. He knows how to help. Or you could hire a housekeeper." She punched his arm lightly. "And I'm positive Chase can tell you what you shouldn't be watching on television."

"You're a real comedian, Beth."

"But you admit you can handle the situation?"

Wyatt tossed his sandwich in the trash can. His sister's news had killed his appetite. "I don't know. Do you need an answer tonight?"

"We have some time before Gerald comes home. Why don't you think about it and let me know? You could start by spending time with Chase. Weekends. School nights."

He rubbed his hand over his face. "I didn't need this right now, Beth."

"Do you think another day would have made a difference, Wyatt?"

"Probably not."

"All I'm asking is that you accept your God-given right to parent the precious son you've been given. Karen would have been proud of Chase."

"I know. He's really something. Did I tell you I watched him at play practice the other day? He's learned most of his lines already. They only had to prompt him a time or two."

"He has an excellent memory. Just like you."

"Yeah, I never forget anything," he agreed, the deeper meaning of his statement evident to them both.

"It's time, Wyatt. Put the past behind you and step into a future with Chase. I promise to be with you as much as possible, but I want Chase to know his dad as I know him. You're a pretty special guy. Let yourself believe that and let him love you. You won't regret it."

Her words humbled him. He looked down at his hands. He could feel the moisture in his eyes when he looked up at her. "How did we get to this? At first it was a couple of years for me to get back on my *feet*. Then he was in school, and I was working those long hours. Then I didn't want to take him from the only home he's ever known. I excused myself from ten years of his life."

"Chase knows you love him, Wyatt. I've shared with him everything I know about you and Karen. I know he's wondered why he didn't live with you, and I've tried to make him understand. Did you know Chase prays for you every night? That one reason he wanted to be in the Easter program was because he hoped you would find God and be happy?"

"What made him think that?"

"Kim mentioned he could help people find Jesus Christ, and you were the person he thought of. And before you blame Kim for that, I want you to know he came up with the idea all on his own."

Wyatt knew it was past time. "Okay, Beth. Do we need to discuss this with Chase?"

She nodded. "I don't want him thinking I'm abandoning him. He needs to make the final decision."

"How about if we plan on Chase spending some time with me each week until Gerald gets home, and then he can move in for the duration of Gerald's leave? We'll look at the situation after that, and if he's unhappy we'll decide what to do then."

Beth hugged her brother. "I think Chase will be happy spending time here. You can do all those manly things with him. He loves Ole Blue, and he's always been fascinated by that deer head over your fireplace. And you can tell him things about his mother I never could."

"It has been a long time since I was this uncertain about something."

"Your confidence level will grow with experience. Stop thinking everything to death. Experience the love of your son."

❧

The plans for the conversation with Chase proceeded quickly. On Friday night Wyatt went over to Beth's, and they ordered pizza.

When Beth brought up the subject of Chase spending time with his Dad, Wyatt steeled himself for a definite no or even tears.

"I'd like that."

Chase's simple response blew him away. How could the child he'd all but abandoned those many years ago want anything to do with him? "Why, Chase?"

The boy's gangly body shifted with his shrug. "You're my dad. All my friends talk about the fun things they do with their dads, so I figure we'd have fun, too. Will you help me build a birdhouse for Miss Natalie?"

The word *help* registered in Wyatt's mind. His son hadn't asked him to build the house but to help. Chase's ability to be so generous in his love rocked Wyatt's world. "We can do that."

Chase smiled. "Can we go to church? Miss Natalie lets me help in her classroom sometimes. She makes neat stuff."

"We'll see."

"I really like church," the boy said.

"I know, Chase. Your aunt has told me."

"Can I watch my movie?" he asked his aunt.

"Yes. Can you watch it in your room? I'd like to talk to your dad."

"Sure. 'Bye, Dad. See you."

Wyatt's gaze followed the boy from the room. "I'm humbled by that kid."

"He knows that you love him, and now he's going to do

something his friends are doing. He's not the rebel you were."

"I bet Mom and Dad love that."

"They love you, Wyatt. They don't always understand you, but they care about what happens to you and Chase. Be thankful Chase isn't like you were, or you'd have had him back in your life much sooner."

"Is that why you want me to step up for the teenage years?" Wyatt teased.

Beth laughed. "Smart, huh?" She glanced toward the bedroom door and lowered her voice. "He might hear us and think the wrong thing."

"He's going to be okay, Beth. You've done a wonderful job, and I promise to do everything in my power to justify that love you've instilled in him."

"What do you think about his spending next Friday night at your place? You could take him fishing. He's never been."

Wyatt's eyes widened. "He's never been fishing?"

"I don't do bait. I'll come to your place for a fish fry and bring him home with me for church."

"Sounds like you've worked this out to your benefit. Of course I certainly need to remedy the fishing situation. He's an Alexander man. He's got to love fishing."

"What if he's too soft-hearted?"

"There's only one way to find out." He called his son's name, and the boy came running.

"How would you like to spend next Friday night with me and go fishing on Saturday?"

Surprise flashed in Chase's expression. He smiled broadly and nodded.

"That's what we'll do then. Bring warm clothes. It's cold on the water this time of year."

"I don't have a pole."

"You can use one of mine, and we'll get you your own if you like fishing."

Chase flung his arms about his dad's neck and hugged him. "Wait until I tell Buddy. He's always talking about his dad."

Wyatt choked up.

"Finish your movie and get ready for bed," Beth directed. "And work on your fishing strategy. I'm expecting to eat lots of fish."

"We'll catch hundreds, won't we, Dad? We can do loaves and fishes like Jesus did."

"Fish can be difficult to catch sometimes," Wyatt warned, all the while hoping his son's first fishing experience would be a good one. "We'll have to take it one step at a time."

❧

With the arrival of March, Kim found herself with frazzled nerves. So many aspects of the play were in place, but the children's inability to commit to the performance drove her crazy.

They hadn't had one practice yet in which all the children with assigned roles were present. She'd reassigned and rearranged roles every week until she could hardly keep track of the changes. At least she could count on Chase Alexander.

She'd been a bit surprised the previous evening when Chase said his dad had brought him to practice. She'd meant to call Beth and ask if everything was okay, but time had slipped away from her.

Ever since Mrs. Allene had come home, she'd been running errands and picking up groceries to help Maggie. She also visited with Mrs. Allene as often as possible to give her friend a break.

Maggie had reached Dillon Rogers, and he'd promised to make arrangements to come home. Maggie had tried to impress upon him that things were pretty bad, but she didn't think he believed her. He'd kept arguing that his mother had told him not to worry.

"I couldn't believe he was being so thickheaded," Maggie

told Kim. "Does he honestly think his mother would say, 'I hate to bother you, but I'm dying—and could you come home?'"

"At least he's coming."

"He'd better make it soon. The doctor doesn't think she'll last long."

Wyatt showed up a few minutes after practice, looking stressed.

"Wyatt? Where's Beth?"

"At home, I suppose."

"Hey, Dad."

Wyatt handed Chase the keys. "Wait for me in the truck. You can play the radio, but don't start the engine. I need to talk with Miss Kim."

The distinct impression he wasn't happy with her gave Kim pause. She hadn't seen or talked to him over the past few days. "I wondered if Beth was sick. Chase told me you brought him to practice."

"Stop beating around the bush," Wyatt snapped. "You want to know what's going on. Ask."

"I don't understand."

"Don't act so innocent. You got what you wanted, Kim. I'm fulfilling my fatherly duties. Chase is living with me part-time."

His hostility shocked her. "What are you talking about? I never—"

"Sure you did. And now that Gerald's about to return stateside I can either accept responsibility for my son or they'll adopt Chase, and maybe I'll see him a couple of times a year."

Kim gasped. "They won't let you see him?"

Wyatt snorted. "It would hardly be practical. Beth is going to live on a military base in Arizona with Gerald."

"Beth's moving?"

"That's what I said."

"She didn't mention it."

Kim would miss having Beth next door, but she understood her friend missed her husband and wanted to be with him. She could tell the change frustrated Wyatt. She wanted to believe Wyatt wanted his son with him or he would never have agreed to Chase's living with him part-time. "So how's it going?"

The look he flashed her spoke volumes. "Just wonderful. Between carting him around to his school, sports, and church activities, I barely have time to do my work. At first it was just Friday night and Saturday, but before that weekend was up Beth decided she wanted him to stay with me more."

He wasn't being fair. It wasn't her fault Beth expected him to spend time with his son. He was just like the others. Confront him with a challenge and he had to find someone else to blame. Chase was his responsibility, not Beth's. "I'm sure things will settle down once you adjust to each other's schedules."

"My life will never be the same. Beth and her meddling friend have made sure of that."

"If you mean me, my name is Kimberly Elliott. I did not meddle in your business. Tell you what, Wyatt—why don't you go home and hide in your precious workshop? I'll make sure Chase gets to and from practice. I wouldn't want you to be inconvenienced because of me."

"Why don't I just take Chase home for good and see what that does for your little play?"

Kim couldn't believe he'd be so cruel. She knew without doubt that none of the other children in the church could do half as well as Chase. The part of her that wanted to throw down the gauntlet fought for dominance, but she restrained herself.

"Chase has worked very hard for this, Wyatt. Don't punish him or the church because you're angry with me."

"I'm not angry with you." Wyatt growled his frustration.

"Well, maybe I'm taking it out on you. I'm ashamed and furious at myself for letting things get so bad. For years I've thought of myself. Sure, I love my son, but it was easy to believe he was better off with Beth. Now I have Chase, and Beth, and you, and even Cornerstone demanding stuff from me I'm not prepared to give."

"Are you talking about the stage?"

"No. The stage is finished. All I have to do is screw it together."

"Then what?" Kim asked. She wanted to understand his confusion, particularly the role he felt Cornerstone played.

"You all expect me to be something I'm not."

"You mean a loving father and good person?"

"That and other stuff. You make me think about being different, and I've been the same for so long I'm not sure I want to change."

"We all change, Wyatt."

"Have you?"

"I've made mistakes in my life," Kim admitted. "And I vowed I'd never make them again. I'm struggling, but I'm getting there."

"But how can you be struggling? You're a good Christian woman. Why would you worry about anything?"

"I want the same things as every woman, Wyatt. A husband, children, a happy home; but I keep making the wrong decisions, and I'm still alone.

"What sort of decisions?"

Kim felt uncomfortable with the question. "I'm attracted to the wrong men."

"What sort of men?" he asked curiously.

"Mostly lying cheaters who aren't looking for the same things I am."

"How do you meet these men? Surely not at church."

"Either I'm a magnet, or there's a sign somewhere on earth

that says if you want a stupid woman, find Kim Elliott." Her pathetic attempt at humor went unnoticed.

"What attracts you to these men?"

"My friends tell me I want to change them. I don't. I couldn't if I tried. But I do see good hearts in them, and maybe they don't intend to hurt me, but they can't help themselves any more than I can. Maybe they believe they're letting me down easy by making me think the worst."

"What do you want in a man?"

Kim shrugged. "Someone good and decent and capable of love, and he has to be a Christian."

"Why?"

"I want to raise my children with my husband."

"Not going to church doesn't mean he wouldn't be there for them."

"How can he guide them to do what's right if he's not willing to do right himself?"

"You don't have to go to church to be a good person."

"But good relationships require things in common with your spouse. The most important thing we'll share is a relationship with our Lord and Savior."

Wyatt just looked at her. Finally he said, "Chase is waiting."

Kim's gaze followed him as he made his escape down the aisle. He glanced back, and she waved good-bye.

"You're doing the right thing, Wyatt," she said softly as the door closed behind him. She glanced upward and whispered, "Thanks."

eleven

Kim had just finished writing up a customer's purchase when the phone rang. "Eclectics. How may I help you?"

"Hi, it's Mari. I wanted to let you know Mrs. Allene died this morning."

Kim felt a knot grow in her throat. "How's Maggie doing?"

"She was with Mrs. Allene. She said she had pretty much slipped into a coma. She didn't think she suffered. She said Mrs. Allene drew one deep breath and passed from this world."

"Where is Maggie now?"

"At her house. She said Dillon Rogers went to the attorney's office to pick up the will. She tried to tell him Mrs. Allene had told her what she wanted for her funeral, but he wouldn't listen. He said they'd talk after he saw the will."

"Why is he being such a jerk?"

"He's grieving, too."

Kim had her own opinion about the man after what Maggie had told her. He'd flown in at mid-morning Tuesday, and from the moment he'd shown up at the house in his rental car he'd treated Maggie like hired help rather than Mrs. Allene's friend.

"I asked Joe about tonight's practice, and he said we should go ahead," Mari said.

"You think everyone will be up to it?"

"We'll miss Mrs. Allene a great deal, but everyone has an investment in the play, too. I feel we should honor Mrs. Allene by forging ahead. Joe agrees."

"I'll be there. I'll probably take a few minutes this afternoon to run by and see Maggie. You want to go with me?"

"Joe and I are going over later this morning."

"What about food?"

"I'm sure the bereavement committee will want to take a meal over to Mr. Rogers tonight."

"You think he'll accept?"

"I pray he's not difficult about accepting the meals *or* the funeral arrangements. Mrs. Allene has been part of Cornerstone all her life. It would be very cruel of him not to allow us to be involved in the services. Joe plans to go over there after Mr. Rogers gets back from the lawyer's office."

"I can't believe he wouldn't listen to Maggie."

Later that afternoon Kim left the store in the hands of her assistant and went over to Maggie's. Kim noted her red eyes as she hugged her friend. "I'm sorry. I know how much you loved Mrs. Allene."

"I'll miss her."

"We all will. What can I do to help?"

"You've helped just by being here."

"You want to come over to the condo and spend the night? Or I could stay here if you want."

"I'm okay. Mari said you're having practice tonight."

"Do you think we shouldn't?"

"Of course not," Maggie declared. "Mrs. Allene was thrilled about the Easter program. She always asked how things were going before she got so sick."

Kim stayed with Maggie until it was almost time to leave for church. She called the store and learned Wyatt had phoned. She dialed the number he'd left. "Hi. Ruby said you called."

"I wondered if you could pick up Chase. I have to finish some cabinets for delivery tomorrow. I'll probably end up working all night."

"I'm at Maggie's. Mrs. Allene died this morning."

"I'm sorry to hear that. Are you having practice?"

"Pastor Joe thinks we should. I'll arrange to have Chase picked up if I can't do it myself. I'm pretty sure the van runs by your place."

"I'm sorry about this, Kim. I already feel like I'm letting Chase down, but I committed to this order before I knew he would be staying with me."

"It's not a problem, Wyatt," she reassured him. "We transport several children to and from church events."

"I'll pick him up if I can break away."

"Just keep working," Kim told him. "I'll make sure he gets home. Did he eat yet?"

Kim could have declared he growled. "No. I forgot."

She glanced at her watch. "Why don't you order a pizza? I'm sure he'd love that."

"Okay. Thanks, Kim."

After ending the call with Wyatt, she dialed the church office and asked that Chase's name be added to the van route for that evening. She returned to the living room to find Maggie paging through a magazine. She doubted her friend even saw the pages. "Wyatt called the store. He needs someone to pick up Chase."

Kim thought about the situation for a few minutes and decided to tell her friend. "Can I talk to you in confidence?"

"Sure. You know it'll never leave the walls of this house."

Kim didn't doubt that for a minute. Maggie was not a gossip. "Wyatt's angry with me. He thinks I had something to do with Beth's asking him to step up and be a father to Chase."

"Did you?"

Kim shook her head. "I may not agree with him missing ten years of his son's life, but I never suggested Beth force Wyatt to take over Chase's care."

"Do you know what's going on?"

"From what I can piece together, Beth's moving to Arizona to live with Gerald on the base. She told Wyatt they would adopt Chase and raise him as their son or he would have to accept his responsibility. Gerald's home on leave, so I haven't had a chance to talk with Beth yet. They're seeing how things work now. I don't want Wyatt to fail at this."

"I'm sure Wyatt doesn't want to fail either."

"He's been alone for so long."

"Be careful, Kim," Maggie cautioned.

"It's already too late. I know it can't work, but I'm involved up to my eyebrows in their lives."

"I came to Cornerstone right after his wife died," Maggie said. "I was still sorting faces and names, but I remember Mrs. Allene getting very upset when people judged Wyatt so harshly. Whenever the subject arose, she reminded them everyone makes mistakes."

"Do you think he's as bad as he tries to make me believe?" Kim asked.

"Could be he wants you to think the worst of him. A good Christian woman showing more than a passing interest in him and his son might be more than he can handle."

"I want what's best for Chase."

"And Wyatt?" Maggie asked.

Kim traced a pattern in the chenille fabric with her finger. "Yes, of course, Wyatt, too. He's so unhappy. He hides it well, but he blames himself for his wife's death."

"I'm sure it became a defining event in his life. Probably even the point where the rebellious boy became a man. He's certainly taken steps forward over the years."

"In everything but family and religion."

"Do you pray for him?"

Kim nodded. "Daily."

"Do you think Wyatt will ever accept Jesus as his Savior?"

"Beth told me Wyatt once said he tried to fool God, and

He took his wife and his foot. I thought she meant he was angry with God, but she says not. He told me he doesn't need a savior."

"But he built the cross and the stage."

"And he's going to frame out the Good Shepherd window," Kim said. "I suspect he's reached a point in his life where he might want to change and doesn't know how."

"He's got a strong witness in his parents and sister. Not to mention his son. I imagine Chase will see to it that his dad comes to church with him."

"If Wyatt can get his schedule under control. He knows Chase is supposed to be at church tonight, but he's tied up on a cabinet order that's due tomorrow. I believe he wants to be a good father but isn't sure what to do about it."

"What do you mean?"

"Like tonight—you should have heard him when I asked if Chase had eaten. He'd forgotten to feed him. I imagine Wyatt has existed on sandwiches, but Chase needs more. He's a growing boy."

"So how can we help?"

"I thought about freezing some dinners to help get them over the rough spots."

"You don't even cook for yourself," Maggie said.

"Because I don't like cooking for one," Kim reminded her.

Maggie nodded. "You want help?"

"Oh, Maggie, this isn't a good time for you."

"I loved Mrs. Allene, and I'll miss her—but one way to get over losses is to jump back into life. I figure I'll take several more days then call the hospital and have them put me back on the schedule. Meanwhile I can make a few meals to help out. Mrs. Allene gave me her macaroni-and-cheese casserole recipe."

"You're kidding?" Mrs. Allene's casserole had always been the congregation's first choice at church dinners.

"She made me promise to keep it secret. I think it would please her to know Chase and Wyatt were enjoying the casserole." They spent a few minutes planning menus. "I have a bag sealer so we can put the food in those and seal them tight."

"What about a cookbook? You think that would help Wyatt?"

"If he had time to cook," Maggie said.

"Beth prepared Chase's snacks. Wonder what he's doing now?"

"I know Natalie would bake him a batch of cookies if you asked. She thinks Chase is a great kid."

"Maybe I will. I'm trying not to involve too many people. I don't want to upset Wyatt." Kim checked her watch. "I suppose I'd better head for church."

"You want company?"

"Sure. We can use all the help we can get."

"Let me comb my hair and grab my purse."

On the way out they discussed the house Maggie rented from Mrs. Allene. "I have no idea what Dillon Rogers will do. Probably sell everything and head overseas again."

"You don't think he'll rent you the house."

Maggie shook her head. "He doesn't strike me as the type who is particularly interested in living at the beach. Although he did say it was good to be home."

"I can imagine a few things about the States are an improvement over a foreign country."

"I don't want to look for another place to live," Maggie said. "But it won't be the same without Mrs. Allene next door either. Mari said the same thing."

The elderly woman had lived between the church parsonage and the home Maggie rented.

"I'll help you look if you have to move."

"It's probably time I consider buying something. Mrs.

Allene gave me a good rent because she was more concerned about someone to take care of the house than making a profit. Anything I find will be much higher. I might as well pay myself."

"Mom and Dad gave me a deal on the condo when I came back to manage the store. It was one of their rental units. I've enjoyed having a place where I can make changes when I want to."

"Did Julie and Noah buy the unit in your building?"

Kim shook her head. "Too expensive. The owner got multiple offers."

"I imagine Julie is tired of Noah's apartment."

Practice went better than expected that night, and Kim praised the Lord. Mrs. Allene's death, along with questions about what Dillon Rogers would do, was on everyone's mind, but that didn't seem to hinder their progress.

When the kids loaded in the van for the trip home, Mr. Simmons asked Kim if she could take Chase home. "I had more kids than usual tonight, and it'll be late when I drop him off."

"I'll take him. I appreciate your picking him up."

"No problem. Great play."

Kim smiled at his encouragement. Everyone in the church seemed determined to offer the positive reinforcement she needed.

Maggie had walked up and stood beside her. "I heard. I'll walk home with Mari. It's possible I'll hear from Dillon Rogers tonight about the plans for Mrs. Allene's funeral. We'll talk tomorrow about what we discussed earlier."

Kim hugged Maggie and called to Chase. After they were in the car she asked, "How do you like staying with your dad?"

"It's okay. He's kind of busy. He's gonna help me build Miss Natalie a birdhouse. She said she wanted one for her yard. One of those with the copper tops like Dad has."

"I'm sure both of you will enjoy that."

"Miss Kim, do you think my dad will come to the play?"

She pulled onto the highway. "I'm sure he'll try."

"Aunt Beth said she'd be there."

"A lot of people will be at the play. Does that frighten you?"

"Sort of. Aunt Beth says I need to ask God to give me strength. She says He'll relieve my fears."

"He will." Kim glanced at him. "I've asked Him to relieve mine, too."

"You're afraid?"

"Sure I am. I try not to worry though. I'm here for you, Chase. I appreciate what you're doing. The play wouldn't be a success without you."

"Aunt Beth says I shouldn't be prideful."

Kim smiled. "It's hard, isn't it? We want praise for a good job, but when you're working for Jesus it's not about praise. We're doing this to show our love for Him."

She parked in the yard, and they met Wyatt coming out of the house with a cup of coffee and a wedge of cold pizza.

Chase called hello to his father and ran inside. Kim wondered what the hurry was. "Did you finish?"

Wyatt shook his head. "I've got hours of staining to do. I need to make sure Chase gets to bed and then go back to work."

"Need an extra set of hands?" When he hesitated, she said, "I know my way around a can of stain."

"If you're sure?"

"I wouldn't offer if I weren't. If you'd like to get started, I'll fix Chase a snack and see that he takes his bath."

"I need to spend a few minutes with him," Wyatt told her. "I've been in the workshop all week. Beth's going to be furious. I promised we'd spend time together."

"I'm sure she understands you had prior commitments. Chase mentioned the birdhouse you're going to help him build. I think he has a crush on Natalie."

Wyatt nodded. "The minute these cabinets are hung, I'll gladly build all the birdhouses he wants."

"Not build," Kim said. "His objective is that you help him."

"I know. I hope he understands this work is what puts food on our table and keeps a roof over our heads. I suppose I'll have to cut back if Chase comes here to live full time. Let me go speak to him."

Kim waited in the kitchen, sipping a cup of the strong coffee he had made and wondering about Wyatt's comment. Surely he wouldn't consider sending Chase away.

Wyatt returned about ten minutes later. "Chase said he'd take a shower after he watches his program. He's going to call the shop when he gets in bed."

"You have a phone out there?"

"Yeah, but we're using his walkie-talkies."

Kim grinned. "I bet he enjoys that."

"Seems to. I have so much to learn. I want to make him happy."

"He's a tween, Wyatt. He's about to undergo a total change."

He held the door open for her. "What's a *tween*?"

Her lack of experience with children had led Kim to read several books on child development to help her in working with the kids at church. "He's no longer a child, and he's not a teen, so they refer to them as *tweens*."

In the shop he found her a smock, safety glasses, and gloves and directed her to the area where he'd set up the cabinets on sawhorses and boards. "Wouldn't it be easier to stain these once you get them in place?" Kim asked.

"I like to control my environment."

Kim nodded. "Okay, show me how you want it done."

After a short lesson on the Wyatt Alexander method of applying stain, she went to work. He watched for a minute and, after a satisfied nod, he himself began staining a cabinet door. "How was practice?"

"Better than I thought. I was afraid everyone would be depressed over Mrs. Allene's death, but they're determined the show must go on."

"Have the arrangements for her funeral been made yet?"

"I suppose her son will make them tomorrow. I pray he allows the church to be involved."

The walkie-talkie crackled to life, and Chase said good night. " 'Night, Chase. Love you."

"Love you, too, Dad. 'Night, Miss Kim."

Wyatt hit the button for Kim to say good night to Chase and returned the unit to the counter. "Dillon will have to do what he's comfortable with. She was his mother."

Kim didn't comment on the father-son exchange, but it pleased her that Wyatt told Chase he loved him. "Mrs. Allene told Maggie what she wanted, and he wouldn't even listen. He had to have a copy of the will. I don't think Mrs. Allene would have put her funeral plans in the will. She's been at Cornerstone all her life. The congregation needs the funeral as much as Dillon Rogers does."

"Why would you say that?"

"He hasn't been in his mother's life for years. The membership has been Allene Rogers's family, too. Look at Maggie. She loved Mrs. Allene enough to take a leave of absence from work and care for her."

He looked stunned. "Without pay?"

"Yes. Maggie and Mrs. Allene grew close when Maggie first moved to the area. Mrs. Allene invited her to church, and Maggie's been there ever since. We're afraid Dillon Rogers will handle things quickly and return overseas. Mrs. Allene deserves better."

"Is he her only family?"

"No. She has cousins and nieces and nephews here as well."

"He'll need to handle the estate before he leaves."

Kim concentrated on staining the cabinet door. After she

finished she asked Wyatt's opinion.

"You do good work."

She grinned at him. "Told you."

"I'd tell you to start another one, but it's nearly ten thirty."

"I probably should get home and check with Maggie to see what plans have been made."

"I appreciate your help."

"Next time ask before the last minute." Kim peeled off the gloves and removed the safety glasses.

"I'll remember that, though I'm going on record as saying there won't be a next time. Chase needs more than a part-time dad. No more last-minute staining jobs. Thanks for bringing him home."

"My pleasure." She hung the smock on a nearby peg and picked up her car keys.

"Kim!" Wyatt called as she started to leave. "Let me know about the funeral."

"I will."

Wyatt's dog raced over when she left the building, barking at her and then pushing his head beneath her hand. Kim greeted him and rubbed his head before unlocking her car door.

What a day it had been. She'd never have thought she'd volunteer to help Wyatt in his workshop, but it hadn't been all bad. At least she'd seen a different side of him. And maybe he'd seen a different side of her.

twelve

"And then he accused me of taking advantage of an old lady," Maggie told Kim and Mari.

Mari had called the store the next morning and suggested they take Maggie out to lunch. She hadn't said much, but Kim suspected something was up.

"After Mari dropped me off, I barely got the lights on before he started pounding on the door. I thought maybe he wanted information for the funeral, but he started throwing out accusations right and left. I had no idea Mrs. Allene had changed her will to leave the rental property to me."

"Has he made any plans for the funeral?" Mari asked.

Maggie shook her head. "None that I'm aware of."

"Joe said he was going to call him today to see what he plans to do."

"Do you think he called yet?" Kim asked.

"I have no idea. He doesn't always share church business with me."

"I don't even care anymore," Maggie announced. "If Dillon Rogers doesn't have a funeral for her, I'm planning a memorial service myself. I won't allow him to hurt the church."

"What will you do about the house?" Kim asked.

Maggie frowned. "I'll worry about that after the funeral is over."

"You think he'll contest the will?"

"He threatened that last night. Then when he had me in tears, he couldn't escape soon enough. I don't think he's very comfortable with sobbing women."

Mari took a sip of her iced tea. "Most men aren't."

"Then they shouldn't make us cry," Kim pointed out.

"I tried to call you, but you weren't home," Maggie said.

"I hung around and helped Wyatt stain cabinets. He had a big order that's due today. I got home around eleven or so and figured it was too late to call."

"I think I finally cried myself to sleep around three." Even as she spoke, her eyes filled with tears.

"Oh, Maggie, I'm so sorry."

The woman rose quickly. "I need to run to the ladies' room. I'll be right back."

Unsure what to do, Kim looked at Mari. "How do we help her?"

"Prayer is the only recommendation I have. It's not fair to judge Dillon Rogers based on his treatment of Maggie."

"He's not being fair," Kim declared. "You know as well as I do that Maggie would never ask Mrs. Allene to change her will. In fact, we were talking about finding her another place to live the same day Mrs. Allene died. She had no idea what Dillon Rogers planned to do with the rental property."

The waitress arrived with their soup and salad. After she left, Mari said, "I'm sure he's shocked by the arrangements his mother made. Maggie's not family or anything."

"She was like a daughter to Mrs. Allene," Kim said.

Mari looked sad. "The idea of people fighting over worldly possessions is so depressing. I was an only child, too, but Mom had very few things to leave me. We sold a lot of it to pay her bills."

Kim reached over to squeeze Mari's hand. She kept forgetting Mari had lost her mother not so long ago. Her mother's death coupled with Mari's own breast cancer diagnosis within such a short time span had thrown their friend for a loop. Everyone had been heartbroken the previous summer when the pastor had announced his wife had cancer. Mari had been blessed with a miracle of physical healing, though, and then had fought her way out of the depression that tried to take control of her life. She'd seemed happier since their Christmas vacation, but she still experienced times of sadness.

"I know it was never Mrs. Allene's plan that Maggie suffer because of the situation. I hope Pastor Joe lets her son know everything Maggie has done for his mother."

"I don't," Maggie said, returning to her seat. "I did what I did out of love for Mrs. Allene, not so she'd leave me a house in her will. I've already decided to sign it back over to him."

"He doesn't understand," Mari said softly.

"Nor does he want to," Kim insisted.

"Don't let your distaste for bad boys color your attitude toward him," Maggie told Kim. "I have to forgive him just as Jesus expects."

Kim felt somewhat miffed by their comments. "I'm not particularly big on forgiving people who intentionally hurt others."

Maggie poured the dressing over her salad and unrolled her silverware. They said grace, and she took a bite before saying, "Hate the deed, not the person, Kim."

"What if you can't separate the person and the deed?"

"Then you need to get to know them better," Mari offered. "We make our initial decision on whether we'll like a person so quickly that we can miss out on special people if we don't take a second look."

"It's still not right," Kim insisted. Laying her fork on the salad plate, she dug around in her purse and pulled out her cell phone. She held it out to Mari. "Will you at least call Pastor Joe and see if he's talked to Dillon Rogers yet?"

"Only so you don't get indigestion," Mari said, smiling, as she punched in the numbers and hit SEND.

"Hi, Jean. Is Joe there? . . . Okay. Thanks. . . . No. I'll talk to him when he gets home."

Mari closed the flip phone and pushed it across the table to Kim. "You'll be happy to know he's gone over to talk with Dillon Rogers."

"That's good, right?" Kim asked, looking at Maggie.

"We'll see. It all depends on what he decides."

The waitress topped off their glasses and asked if they wanted dessert.

Kim ordered a hot fudge brownie. Mari and Maggie opted to pass. "You know you'll want something when you see mine," Kim told them, grinning.

"True. Bring three forks," Maggie told the waitress.

Their laughter seemed to relieve the heaviness of their earlier conversation.

"Maggie's coming over to the house this afternoon to help with the costumes."

"I thought those were finished."

"They were until you added five more children."

Kim shrugged. "What's a director to do? If they come, they must be in the play."

"We can always use audience members," Mari suggested. "I don't think you can add another thing to the play without going back to Adam and Eve."

Kim giggled. "That sounds more like a miniseries. I've been thinking we need more practices. I wonder how Pastor Joe would feel about putting the stage in place the week of the play so we can practice in the sanctuary."

"Joe would work around us, but the congregation might not look favorably on having the church pieces removed for regular services."

"True. But I was thinking the children need to become familiar with the stage so they don't trip or fall."

"You should ask Joe. He's probably already anticipated this anyway."

After they sampled the dessert and talked for a few minutes

longer, Kim grabbed her bag. "Well, ladies, business calls. Have fun."

"Want us to come by later and help you find those pewter pieces for the play?" Mari asked.

"I took care of that on Monday. I got nervous when someone asked how much the pieces were. I told them they would be on sale after Easter."

"You are a nut," Maggie said.

"That's salesperson extraordinaire to you."

Back at the store Kim found herself feeling a little out of sorts when she considered Maggie's chastisement of her attitude toward Dillon Rogers. Of course, Maggie had a point when she'd said hate the deed. Her anger had to do with his mistreatment of her friend. She didn't know the man well enough to judge him.

The afternoon passed slowly. A few lookers came in and left with empty hands while others returned to purchase items they'd seen on previous trips. Despite the activity she was playing computer games when the phone rang around four o'clock.

"Busy?" Maggie asked.

"I wish. Did you and Mari finish the costumes?"

"Until you add more children."

"No more kids. I have to draw the line somewhere."

"Good idea. You've single-handedly turned fabric stores into the area's number-one business."

Kim laughed. "Not with those deals Mari's been getting. Are you feeling better?"

"Yes. Joe called home and told Mari the funeral is Saturday morning at the church. The visitation will be at the funeral home Friday night, and a luncheon for the family will be held following the service. Dillon doesn't want any visitation at the house, nor does he want anyone bringing food over."

"At least that's something. Has the bereavement committee

started planning for the luncheon?"

"I put you down for ham. I'm making the macaroni-and-cheese casserole. I'm making extra for Chase and Wyatt."

"And I'll get extra ham. That goes well with mac and cheese."

"I need to run. Dillon asked for my help in identifying his mother's favorite dress."

"Is he treating you better?" Kim asked.

"I think Joe might have told him he should talk to me about the plans. Mrs. Allene had told Joe during one of his visits that I knew what she wanted."

"I'll talk to you tonight then."

Kim felt relieved for Maggie's sake. She knew her friend would have been heartbroken if Dillon Rogers had left her out of the arrangements.

She ran by the grocery store after work to pick up ham and a few more items. After she put away the food Kim picked up the phone and dialed Wyatt's number. He answered on the third ring.

"Did you get the cabinets installed?"

"With minutes to spare. The contractor hinted he'd like to put more business my way. I said we'd talk."

That didn't strike her as cutting back, which was what Wyatt had said he would do. "I called to let you know Mrs. Allene's funeral is Saturday morning."

"Flowers or contributions?"

"I didn't even think to ask. I just got the time of the funeral late this afternoon."

"I'll check tomorrow's paper. I'm sure the obituary will say. Are you feeling better now that the plans have been made?"

Kim considered his question and told the truth. "I'm struggling with Dillon Rogers's treatment of Maggie."

"You mean about the funeral plans?"

"And the will," Kim said. "Mrs. Allene left Maggie the

rental property she lives in. He didn't take that news well."

"I imagine not," Wyatt said. "Don't you think he's entitled to feel upset? His inheritance has been given to a stranger."

Kim wasn't happy Wyatt agreed with Dillon's behavior.

"Maggie wasn't a stranger. Mrs. Allene wanted Maggie to have the house. I don't believe he should question his mother's decision."

"He can't be sure Maggie didn't influence her."

"That's a terrible thing to say. How can you even suggest something like that?"

Wyatt sighed. "I've never met your friend, Kim. I can't tell you what she's like. Mrs. Allene's son can't either."

"You men are all alike. And you have met Maggie. She bought a piece of furniture from you."

Wyatt grunted his irritation. "Don't get upset because I don't agree with you about this. I'm entitled to my opinion, too."

"Not if that opinion is based on total disregard for my friend," Kim snapped back. "I'll have you know Maggie never expected one thing in return. Maggie showed Mrs. Allene Christian love. She's already said she'll sign the house back over to him before she'll argue the point."

"Then it won't be a problem."

"If Mrs. Allene wanted Maggie to have the house, she should have it," Kim persisted. "Oh, why am I arguing with you about this? You can't begin to understand how Maggie feels about the man's attacks on her."

"If anyone understands attacks, I should," Wyatt countered. "You pounce on me every time I disagree with something you say."

"I do not."

"Then why don't I feel the love right now?"

She couldn't win. "Forget it. I only called to tell you about the funeral."

"And I appreciate that," Wyatt said. "I also appreciated your help last night. I thought maybe Chase and I could stop by later and finalize the measurements for your kitchen if you have time."

"Are you sure you want to come into enemy territory?"

"I can handle it if you can. We'll be there around eight."

Wyatt and Chase showed up right on time.

"We brought something to sweeten you up," Wyatt said, handing her a white bakery bag. "Sorry. They were hot when we got them. We ate ours at the store."

She looked inside to find a couple of warm doughnuts. "Thanks." She turned to his son and asked, "Did you enjoy the doughnuts, Chase?"

"Yes, Miss Kim. Dad picked me up from school, and we worked on plans for the birdhouse. Dad says measurements are important. He said to measure twice. . . ." His voice trailed off, and he glanced at his father.

"Cut once," Wyatt prompted.

"Yeah, that's it. I'm going to help Dad with the measurements for your cabinets. He said I might be able to help build them in the shop."

"Good for you." She glanced at Wyatt. "Unless you need a third pair of hands, I'll leave you to your work."

"We'll shout if we do. Oh, do you have measurements on the new appliances you picked out?"

"They're in the folder on the counter. You'd better get busy. It's nearly Chase's bedtime."

"We probably should have waited until tomorrow night. He stays up an hour later on Friday and Saturday."

Kim ripped off a paper towel and grabbed the doughnuts on her way out of the kitchen.

Her awareness of the two males in her home was strong, but Kim forced herself to remain focused on the program she was watching. She refused to stand around looking at Wyatt work.

Her glass of soda sat on the end table. She opened the bag

and dug inside for her favorite, a plain glazed. Kim took a bite and savored the doughnut.

It seemed their earlier argument had rolled right off Wyatt's back. Why couldn't she forget as easily? The anger she felt at injustices was not what God intended for her. He wanted her to forgive and forget as Maggie had told her.

Finally Kim gave up on the program and walked over to the kitchen door. Chase chattered nonstop as he held the tape measure while his father read and jotted down measurements.

"We're nearly finished," Wyatt said when he noticed her.

"No rush. Do you think I'll be able to get the cabinets I wanted in here?"

"Maybe even a couple more." He tapped the pad on the counter. "I'll take these back to the shop and draw up a plan. Did you want them all the way to the ceiling or dropped so you can display items across the top?"

"Dropped. I have lots of stuff to display."

"You may have to have some of the ceiling redone once the soffit is removed."

Kim nodded, watching Chase as he tried to use the tape measure without his dad's assistance. "Your helper is waiting on you."

"Poor guy's done enough of that lately. I hope I can dedicate the time he deserves now that I have that last project out of the way."

He wrote the last number on the paper. "That's it, buddy. We're finished." He held up the folder. "Mind if I take this with me?"

"You think I should buy the appliances now?"

Wyatt shook his head. "I'd wait. They look to be fairly standard-sized. If you can't get these specific units, you should be able to get others that fit. Chase, let's get out of here so Miss Kim can call it a night."

"Thanks, Wyatt. You, too, Chase. Your dad is gaining an

excellent assistant. Do you have a minute, Wyatt? I'd like to speak with you privately."

"Can I run next door and pick up my books?" Chase asked then.

"I don't want you going into the condo without me." He glanced at Kim. "Beth and Gerald went on a short cruise."

Kim nodded. She had been watering Beth's plants while they were away.

"Finish rolling up the tape, and then we'll get your books."

They walked down the hall to her door. Kim shifted uncomfortably. "I'm sorry. I keep jumping to Maggie's defense, and she doesn't want me doing that. I guess she recognizes how weak I am when it comes to forgiving others."

Wyatt's expression was one of understanding. "I'm not your enemy, Kim. I only want you to consider both sides of the story. You know your friend, but you didn't even consider the fact that Mrs. Allene's son doesn't. His mother was an elderly sick woman living alone. Those are prime targets for people who take advantage of others."

"But he judged Maggie without giving her an opportunity to defend herself. Don't you think Mrs. Allene mentioned her friend Maggie in the telephone calls and letters to her son?"

"Maybe, but could be he thought Maggie was his mother's age. Then when he arrived and found her to be much younger and a beneficiary in his mother's estate, I'm sure doubts arose in his mind."

His logic made sense. "I'm sorry I jumped on your case."

Their gazes locked as Wyatt reached to tuck a stray lock of hair behind her ear. "I admire your loyalty to your friends. I'd like to be numbered among that group."

"You are. I admire you for what you're doing, too, Wyatt. I know Chase's happiness means a lot to you."

The intimacy of their conversation struck Kim as Wyatt leaned forward. She placed her hand against his chest. "Don't.

We can't do this."

He covered her hand with his. "Why not?"

"I made a vow to God. I won't make another mistake."

"What if it's not a mistake?"

Before she could respond, Chase came out of the kitchen, waving the tape. "I'm finished. Ready, Dad?"

Wyatt looked at Kim and nodded.

"See you at church, Miss Kim."

Kim hugged the child. "Thanks again."

"Got one of those for me?" Wyatt asked.

She hugged him and stepped away quickly.

What am I doing? Kim asked herself after closing and locking the door. Allowing Wyatt and Chase Alexander to get under her skin didn't bode well for her heart. Kim knew without a doubt she could never again accept a man who believed he didn't need God in his life.

If anyone needed God's grace it was Wyatt Alexander. He needed to accept that he was forgiven and get on with the major task of raising his son in a Christian home.

She could only pray that one day Wyatt would come to know the full extent of God's grace in his life and learn to depend on His Son rather than himself.

thirteen

The funeral for Allene Rogers became a celebration of her life. So many words of comfort were spoken not only to her son and other family members but also to the members of the congregation who had loved the woman and been loved in return.

Pastor Joe's sermon touched on the woman he'd known for a short time, and eulogies from those who had known her much longer were a true reflection of the woman's impact on so many lives over the years.

No one had been more surprised than Kim when Wyatt came into the church and sat down next to her on Saturday morning.

The service started out with the congregation singing "Amazing Grace," and as the words to the song filled her heart Kim found her awareness of Wyatt standing next to her, singing from the same hymnal, nearly overwhelming.

Maggie stood on her other side, her voice cracking with emotion as she sang the words. Kim suffered for her, knowing how difficult this must be.

Mrs. Allene was interred next to her husband in the church cemetery. Afterward Wyatt invited Kim to lunch, but she told him she had to help with the funeral luncheon. She needed to distance herself from him.

"You can come, too, Wyatt," Maggie said. "There's more than enough food for anyone who wants to pay tribute to Mrs. Allene."

Thanks, Maggie, Kim thought as they walked into the fellowship hall. Pastor Joe and Dillon Rogers stood inside the door. They shook Dillon's hand and offered their sympathy.

"I'm so sorry about your loss, Mr. Rogers," Kim said.

She found his smile much like Mrs. Allene's. "Call me Dillon."

Wyatt shook his hand. "Your mom was quite a woman."

"Mom set a real example for me. Too bad I wasn't a good son when she needed me most."

Wyatt glanced at Kim. "I doubt she would have wanted it to be any different," he said when Kim didn't speak.

"I need to help get the food on the table," Kim said hastily. "I'm truly sorry about your mother. She will be missed."

Kim left Wyatt and Dillon talking and went to find Maggie. "He's kicking himself for not being there when his mother needed him."

"He shouldn't do that," Maggie said softly.

Kim looked at her. "Yes, he should. He should have come home sooner."

"Mrs. Allene didn't want that, Kim. I'm sure he would have come if she'd called when this started, but she didn't. Besides, who are we to judge Dillon Rogers? I saw Mrs. Allene often and had no idea how sick she was. If we're assigning blame, my name should be at the top of the list."

"That's not so," Kim pointed out. Why was Maggie trying to shoulder all the blame? It was true Mrs. Allene should have told her son the seriousness of her illness, but other family members should have looked out for her. "No one did more for Mrs. Allene than you."

"She was a dear friend. I'll miss her."

"You can't blame yourself for her death," Kim insisted.

Wyatt walked over to stand beside Kim. "She's right. No one had the ability to change the way things happened. God is in control."

Kim couldn't have been more surprised by Wyatt's words. "Exactly my point," she said, glancing at him. "She thinks she should have noticed sooner that Mrs. Allene was sick because she's a nurse."

"Sometimes we're blinded to the truth when it comes to those we love," Wyatt said. "Or they hide things from us so we don't suffer with them."

Maggie smiled and rested her hands on their arms. "I love you both for the comfort you're offering. I know I couldn't have changed the situation. God was ready to take Mrs. Allene to her glorious home going, and no amount of wishing on my part will change that. I wouldn't bring her back if I could. She's in a much better place. I pray she's already met my family and told them I know the Lord. That would make them so very happy."

Kim hugged Maggie close as the tears flowed.

"Come on, ladies," Wyatt said somewhat stiffly. "Your guests are waiting. We need to get this food out there."

Maggie sniffed and dabbed her nose with the delicate handkerchief she carried. "You're right. Mrs. Allene wouldn't want us crying our eyes out at the celebration of her life."

After Maggie walked away, Wyatt rested his arm about Kim's shoulders. "Are you okay?"

"Just sad for Maggie."

"But happy for Mrs. Allene?"

Kim nodded. "We always miss those people who impact our lives."

Wyatt looked deep into her eyes. "I know I'd miss you if you weren't around."

Kim felt herself growing warm. She turned quickly and grabbed the platter of sliced ham. "I'd better get this on the table."

Wyatt took it from her hands. "Let me carry that for you."

What was he doing? Kim wondered as he moved into the dining area. If she didn't know better, she'd say Wyatt Alexander was pursuing her. She needed to make sure he understood where they stood. She could never marry a man who didn't know the Lord. Marry? Kim frowned. Where had that come from? Wyatt was just being a good friend. Wasn't he?

                                        ❧

As the days passed, Kim wondered if they would be prepared on time. No doubt the show would go on, but her confidence level seemed to take a nosedive with the weekly practices. Surely nothing had to be as difficult as it seemed.

Kim strongly suspected this was the very reason the church had never varied from tradition on their plays. The traditional plays were so much simpler.

But she refused to be defeated. A friend from church always said she needed to pray a little harder when things got her down. So Kim did exactly that.

Beth and Gerald had returned from their cruise, and Chase remained with his father. She knew Beth missed the child a great deal, but she felt optimistic that father and son would be okay.

Kim ran into Beth on the breezeway in front of their condos and stopped to catch up on the news. Gerald had left for the base in Arizona, and Beth decided not to take any action until she knew something more definite.

"Once we find a place there, I can rent the condo on a weekly basis and still have a place to stay when I come home for vacations," Beth told her.

"That's a good plan. I'm sure the money will come in handy once you start a family."

"Oh, Kim, does change ever frighten you?" Beth asked. "I want to be with Gerald, but moving across the country to a new area and leaving my family behind frightens me. How can I not be there for Wyatt and Chase?"

"Change frightens me, too," Kim agreed. "I know it's difficult, but I think they'll be okay. I've seen the two of them together several times lately, and they're getting along well."

"Chase tells me you've provided food for him and his dad. Is there something else on the horizon for Wyatt and Chase?"

"No. Those meals were mine and Maggie's way of helping Wyatt and Chase adjust. As you know I promised God I would never involve myself with a non-Christian man again, and that's one promise I'm determined to keep."

"Is your heart listening to what your head is saying?"

"I'm struggling, Beth."

"I've noticed a change in him, Kim. If you'd asked me a few weeks ago I would have said you'd never see Wyatt in a church. Since I've been home I've seen him at Chase's practices, as I'm sure you have. He's not dropping him off either. He's sitting in the audience and watching. He's very proud of Chase's portrayal of Jesus."

"I hope for his sake that he can find the happiness God promises him."

"What about you? If Wyatt became a Christian, would you feel differently about him?"

"I care a great deal about Wyatt. I consider him a good friend."

"Just a friend?"

Kim found that question difficult to answer. She wanted to answer with an unequivocal yes, but Wyatt Alexander had begun to play much too large a role in her thoughts for that. She'd gone so far as to ask herself the same question Beth had asked, but her vow kept her from being tempted to give things a try. "That's all it can be," Kim said with a determined nod of her head.

"I admire your strength. Too many women become involved with men, believing they'll change them, only to find it never works."

"I've been right there with those women," Kim said. "Wyatt needs to accept God's forgiveness and forgive himself so he can move on with his life."

Kim knew Beth surely felt her confusion. A truly committed woman would put Wyatt out of her life. She wouldn't talk about keeping vows and regularly place herself in the path of temptation. Wyatt Alexander was beginning to mean too much to her, and Kim knew she had to take action soon or she'd be in over her head.

"I can't believe the play is this weekend. Where did the time go?" Beth asked, changing the subject.

"The older I get, the faster the years seem to go by. Are you coming to dress rehearsal Thursday night?"

Beth nodded. "I'm helping in the back, getting them into their costumes."

"The rehearsal will be the true indicator of what will happen. Pray the children understand how important this is."

"I have."

❧

As Kim expected, five of her key players didn't show up for the dress rehearsal. "Where are they? I specifically told each of them they needed to be here tonight."

"Maybe we need to assign volunteer staff to make sure the key players are here," Julie suggested.

"Oh, they'll be here for the play," Kim said. "It's almost as if they think they don't need the practice."

"Could be they have homework or family activities."

"They're probably home watching television or something."

"You're on edge tonight," Julie said.

"I'm terrified everything will fall apart."

"God won't let that happen, Kim. He gave you this play, and He'll use it for His glory."

"I hope so. For now, though, we'd better do something about the missing actors."

Kim reassigned the roles to willing volunteers, keeping a list in case she needed to do the same the following night.

She walked into the sanctuary to find Wyatt and the other

men putting the stage in place. "I thought you were going to do that tomorrow."

"We thought rehearsal should be as true to the actual performance as we could make it," Pastor Joe said.

"We put the long narrow table in the choir bay for the Lord's Supper scene and the cross in the baptismal," Noah told her. "I stood on it, and it seems sturdy enough."

"Avery and Natalie put their stone wall in place," Pastor Joe said, indicating the area with a nod of his head.

"Julie said you had the sanctuary looking like Bethlehem at Christmas," Noah pointed out. "This surely has to be Jerusalem."

"It's wonderful," Kim said. "A theatrical group couldn't have done better."

"And with God in the mix, it's going to be a soul-winning night."

"Pray with us, Pastor Joe," Kim said.

He led them in prayer, and then the group scattered to their various assignments. Noah would work the lights while their music minister, Rob, controlled the music and sound effects.

"Are you staying?" Kim asked when Wyatt lingered at her side.

"I want to see how the stage holds up under the kids."

She thought of what Beth had said about Wyatt watching his son and figured Chase was the reason he wanted to hang around. "You can be our audience. Let me know if you have any suggestions to improve the performance."

Kim walked up front to address the group of children that had assembled in the front pews of the sanctuary. "Okay, kids. As far as we're concerned, tonight is the first night of the performance. You need to be very careful with your costumes and props. We won't have time to replace anything that gets damaged.

"When we move to the back, you need to remember the audience will be able to hear you, so remain very quiet. I know that's asking a lot, but this is important. I also need silence so I can hear where we are with the lines and know when to move forward.

"Mr. Stevens is making a video of our performance tonight, and we'll watch it afterward while we eat our snack. Pastor Joe, would you like to share a few words of encouragement with the children?"

"I think we have a fine group of actors and actresses here, Miss Kim. I know they're going to do the Lord and Cornerstone proud. If you'll all bow your heads, we'll start with a word of prayer."

Afterward the children moved to the hallway behind the pulpit area. Over in the far corner was another small stage where the narrator would stand.

On stage Mary, Joseph, and the baby Jesus were illuminated in the spotlight, and the star of the East shone in the background. Robin, their narrator, passed her microphone over to little Missy Reynolds, and the music started. Kim felt chill bumps when the child's voice soared with the words of "Away in a Manger."

She slipped into the back and turned on the baby monitor Mari had brought along. The other unit was on the narrator's podium.

The song ended, and Robin began to speak, sharing the passage of time from Jesus' birth until the beginning of His ministry.

"Jesus is coming. Jesus is coming."

She knew from the chanting that the smaller children had just entered with Chase following them. Kim wanted so badly to step out and watch the program but knew it was more important she stay put. Tomorrow night's performance would require her to see from behind closed doors.

Mari walked along with the children lined up in the back area, shushing the children as the volume increased.

Kim found herself holding her breath as scene after scene unfolded. Chill bumps raced along her arms as Robin shared stories of the grace their Lord and Savior bestowed on so many people.

They made it through most of the scenes with minor incidents. Before she knew it, the disciples filed through the choir room door and sat down at the table for the Last Supper.

When Chase spoke his line about one of them betraying him, another child gasped and cried, "Who?"

The sound of laughter came over the speaker.

Bryan, the boy who had bullied the children in an earlier practice, said, "Silly, you're supposed to ask, 'Is it me?'"

"Miss Kim says the line is, 'Is it I, Lord?'" another child corrected.

"She didn't."

"It's Judas," another child volunteered, and the argument started.

Kim stepped into the sanctuary and confronted the unruly children. "Why can't you get this one line right?" she demanded. "'Is it I, Lord?'" she repeated. "What's so difficult about that?" One of the smaller children laughed, and she whirled about. "This isn't funny. It's very serious. Jesus is about to be betrayed."

The child looked as if she were about to cry.

Mari stepped into the sanctuary. "Kim, why don't you take a break now?"

Tears welled in Kim's eyes as embarrassment overwhelmed her. "I'm sorry." She ran out the door without looking back.

Kim went out to her car and sat down in the passenger seat. Once they started, the tears wouldn't stop. Here she was, a day away from the final program, with a group of kids who couldn't repeat one little line properly. She needed a miracle.

She heard a tap on the window and looked up into Wyatt's face. Kim felt even more embarrassed by his presence. He opened the door and passed her a handful of tissues. "Are you okay?"

She managed a teary response. "Obviously not. I just made an idiot of myself."

"They're kids, Kim. They'll give you everything they have to give, but when the urge to play strikes they forget everything else. They were trying to figure out what to say."

Kim sniffed. "That never should have happened. I have no right doing this."

"It's pre-performance jitters. You want things so perfect that you got upset when things went wrong."

She flipped down the visor and lifted the mirror cover. "I'm a mess. Those poor kids will think I've lost my mind if I go back in there with raccoon eyes."

He lifted her chin and looked at her face. "You don't look so bad. Go to the ladies' room and freshen up. I'll let Mari know you're coming back."

"I'm so embarrassed," Kim said as she climbed out of the car.

Wyatt took her hand in his. "Everything will be fine. You shouldn't get so worked up though. It's not good for you."

"It definitely makes me look foolish."

Back in the sanctuary the performance stopped when Kim entered the room. She could sense everyone's eyes focused on her. "I'm sorry. I owe everyone here an apology, particularly those of you playing disciples. Please forgive me."

Pastor Joe stood and came over and placed his arm about her shoulders. "We know how stressed you are. Right, children?"

The chorus of yesses made her feel even guiltier. Had she forgotten the reason she had chosen the children? "I never meant for anyone to suffer because of my determination to succeed."

"We appreciate that determination, Miss Kim," Pastor Joe

told her. "Your dedication to our success means God will reap the benefits. And we all agree we need to remember how serious this part of the story of Jesus' death is. Right, kids?"

Another roar of yesses resounded.

"Why don't we go over the scene again to reassure Miss Kim?" He guided her over to the pew, and she sat down. "And if anyone feels overwhelmed just raise your hand, and we'll stop."

"Thanks, Pastor Joe." She looked at the children, sensing their apprehension and desire to make things right. "You're all doing an excellent job. I know the play will be a big success. Please don't hold my behavior against me. I had no right to act like a baby. I need a big pacifier."

The children laughed and moved back into place as the lights were adjusted.

Kim suspected it was more the other adults' coaching than her outburst that made the scene better. There was only one "Was it me, Lord?" in the bunch, and that came from a fill-in disciple. When Bryan said something to the child, an adult quickly interceded.

"Perfect!" Kim called to them as she rose from the pew. "Let's keep going."

They watched the video in the fellowship hall over snacks, and Kim realized things weren't as bad as they seemed. After the van had left to take the children home, the adults sat, discussing the play.

"I think that went well," Pastor Joe said.

"After I got myself under control," Kim agreed with a sad smile.

Wyatt sat next to her and reached over to squeeze her hand. "We all understand how important this is to you, Kim. You have a major investment in the play. When I build something, I'm always on edge until the buyer says it's exactly what he wants."

"I'm the same way about my sermons," Pastor Joe agreed.

"He is," Mari confirmed. "He goes over them time and time again, asking if something makes sense and if I understand where he's going with the message."

"Giving of ourselves is important," Maggie said. "Wanting the children to perform at their best isn't wrong."

"But yelling at them is," Kim countered. "I appreciate your understanding, but please don't make excuses for my behavior. I owe you all an apology. Not only did I scream at the children, but I did it in God's house. Two no-no's. I need to ask God's forgiveness."

"I'm sure He's already forgiven you," Mari told her. "All in all, I think the rehearsal went well. Don't you?"

"I'm pleased with how it progressed," Kim said. "I think the audience will be in awe of the children's performances. I know I am."

"Tomorrow is the day," Pastor Joe said. "The costumes and props are wonderful. Not to mention the sound effects. Those driving nails are the worst. And the thunder and lightning scene couldn't be more realistic. Let's pray that God will bless our program."

Everyone bowed their heads as Pastor Joe led them in prayer.

After the pastor's "amen," Wyatt said, "I guess I'd better go see if Chase managed to get out of his costume."

"Thanks," Kim said when he squeezed her shoulder. "I appreciate your kindness."

"We all have our moments, Kim. Doesn't mean we're bad people. Just given to human failings."

"Amen," Pastor Joe agreed.

fourteen

Good Friday dawned clear and sunny, and Kim couldn't help but hope the weather was a sign of God's blessing on their performance. She sat on the balcony, enjoying the serene blues and roar of the ocean as she drank her orange juice.

She went to the store for a couple of hours but took the remainder of the day off to finalize last-minute details.

She was at the condo when her parents arrived around three. "It's so good to have you both here," Kim declared as she hugged her mother and then her father.

"You're nervous," her mom said.

Kim smiled and nodded. "Very. This is it. Good or bad, the play is over tonight."

"And God will bless this work, Kim. His work. I know He will."

"He already has. There's time for you and Daddy to take a nap if you want. I have sandwich meats in the fridge. You know where everything is. Help yourself."

"But where are you going?" her mother asked.

"Back to church. I wanted to make sure you arrived safely."

"You're a good daughter." Her mother kissed her on the cheek.

As Kim sat in the sanctuary, viewing the scenery, the full wonder of how things had come together dawned on her. God truly was in control. Not only had He given her the idea for the play, but He'd given her the people to bring that idea to fruition.

Every costume sewn and every prop built were the result of a dedicated friend who desired success for God's work. Their efforts assured Kim she would see her play at its best. Even the children were determined to excel in their performances. That knowledge enveloped Kim in peace. God would make it happen.

"I knew you'd be here," Pastor Joe said.

She smiled at him. "I can't stay away." She picked up the realistic loaf of plastic bread she'd found earlier that day. "Take a look at this."

He turned it over in his hands and shook his head in amazement. "Not even the kids can destroy this. Of course, Chase is going to have a difficult time breaking it in two."

"I have a real loaf for that. I just thought this would look good on the table. I bought some artificial grapes, too."

"You've handled every detail. I'm impressed."

"And I've seen a side of myself I'm not particularly thrilled with," Kim told him.

"Do you think you're the only person to lose control?"

"Well, no. But that doesn't make it all right."

"God is pleased with you, Kim. You may have hurt some people, but you returned and sought their forgiveness. That's what God expects us to do."

"But what if they don't want to come back because of that?"

"Has anyone indicated that? Have any parents called?"

"Well, no," she admitted.

"I know that God plans to bless Cornerstone greatly this weekend."

She was relieved to hear him say so, then followed his gaze to the wall draped in white fabric. "Is it in place?"

Pastor Joe nodded. "The plan is to drop that curtain at the sunrise service on Easter morning."

She let out a breath and smiled. "God is so good."

"His grace is more than sufficient," Pastor Joe agreed.

A few minutes later, her heart swelled with pride as the

excited children began to enter the building. Just as she expected, every child with an assigned speaking role was present. Kim felt disappointed for the stand-ins but knew that was the way of performances.

She'd reward them in the future. Meanwhile, tonight they would become part of the crowds that surrounded Jesus.

Kim gulped when Wyatt and Chase entered the room, Wyatt looking very handsome in his dark suit. "Beth's picking up Gerald at the airport, and then she'll stop by for Mom and Dad."

"Gerald's flying in for the play?"

"For Easter actually, but he came a couple of days early so he could see Chase perform." He squeezed his son's shoulder and smiled down at him.

"You'd better get into your first costume," Kim said.

Chase nodded and walked over to where Mari distributed costumes and waited in line.

"Break a leg," Wyatt told her.

"I'm so nervous," she said, holding out a trembling hand to demonstrate.

Wyatt took it in his. "Worse than Chase, and he has big shoes to fill tonight."

"That he does. Let's pray for him," Kim suggested.

She could tell Wyatt was uncomfortable, but he bowed his head as she prayed for God to work His miracles tonight for all the children's success and particularly Chase.

After saying, "amen," Kim looked up, and Wyatt winked at her.

"Let me get out of here so you can prepare."

He walked over to where Chase stood and spoke to his son. The boy flashed him a broad smile.

After Wyatt left the room, her curiosity got the best of her, so she asked Chase, "What did your dad say?"

"That I'd do Jesus proud."

Kim felt humbled by Wyatt's words to his son.

"You already have," Kim assured. "You've done your best, and that's all anyone, including God, asks."

"Thanks, Miss Kim."

She hugged him and smiled.

Over the next few minutes, confusion and chaos reigned as the adults focused on preparing the children for their roles.

"If anyone needs to visit the bathroom, go now," Kim said. "Once we get started, we'll go straight through. No bathroom breaks or do-overs tonight."

Natalie laughed at Kim's comment as she helped an angel into her costume.

"Did you sew these by hand?" Kim asked, running her finger along the sequin-covered wing straps. "I couldn't believe it when Mari said you'd glued feathers to the wings."

"I had some extra time on my hands. And a couple of extra feather pillows," she added. "What do you think of the stones?"

"I'm impressed."

"By the stones?" she asked curiously. "Or the fact that Avery and I worked together on the project?"

"Both."

"You'll never know the sacrifices I made for your success."

"God's success," Kim corrected. "He loves you for every effort you've made on His behalf."

Pastor Joe rushed into the back. "It's standing room only out there. We're gathering chairs from the classrooms for the aisles."

Kim smiled at Wyatt as he followed the pastor. "You're going to lose your seat."

He shook his head. "Beth's saving me one in the front row."

"All that advertising must have paid off. I heard it on the Christian radio station today," Mari said from across the room.

Maggie finished tying the belts on the smaller children. "I

imagine the nursery is full, too. I'd better go see if they need more help."

"I asked when I dropped off the twins," Mari said. "They had it covered."

The drama team rushed around, getting everyone dressed and lined up according to his or her role.

"Look at me, Miss Kim," Bryan said, holding out his arms to reveal the colorful costume. "I look like Peter in the storybook."

"You certainly do." The fact that he stood at least a head taller as he spoke about the costume told Kim she'd made a good choice.

Mari walked along the row, shushing the rowdier kids. They had no idea how their voices carried.

Kim's butterflies took over when she heard Pastor Joe speaking to the congregation and visitors.

"We'd like to take this opportunity to welcome everyone to tonight's performance. For those of you who are first-time visitors, welcome to Cornerstone Community Church. We know without a doubt that you will be blessed by the performance of *Except for Grace*.

"The play was written by our very own Kimberly Elliott. She's been a member of Cornerstone since she was as young as some of the children you'll see performing tonight. We're doubly blessed to have the children and youth who have dedicated their time over the past few months to make this program a success.

"And now a couple of housekeeping matters." He told the audience how a child's number from the nursery might pop up on the big screens to alert the parents they were needed and then gave directions to the bathrooms.

"And now," he said, the lights going down and a drum roll sounding, "Cornerstone Community Church presents *Except for Grace*."

As the scenes unfolded, each child spoke his or her lines with such clarity that Kim knew God was directing them. The knot in her throat competed with the moisture in her eyes as she listened to Chase say his lines perfectly. She knew hearts were being touched in that audience tonight. Hers certainly was.

It seemed the hours of practice culminated in just a few minutes. Kim shivered as the play reached the part where Jesus died on the cross while thunder rolled and lightning illuminated the darkened room. The sound effect of the curtain being rent in two could be heard throughout the building.

Jesus' body was taken from the cross and moved to the stone tomb. Chase crawled from the tomb into the choir bay and came into the back to change into his white robe while the angel comforted the women at the tomb.

There was yet another audible gasp in the congregation when Chase reappeared high in the baptismal, his arms stretched out as he spoke Jesus' words from the Gospel of Matthew.

" 'Go ye therefore, and teach all nations, baptizing them in the name of the Father, and of the Son, and of the Holy Ghost: teaching them to observe all things whatsoever I have commanded you: and, lo, I am with you always, even unto the end of the world. Amen.' "

Applause filled the room, and the adults quickly organized the children and moved them on to the stage to take a bow.

"Let's give them all another hand," Pastor Joe exclaimed with a broad smile. "Kimberly Elliott, our author and director, and the cast of *Except for Grace*."

They bowed again.

"Tonight we've been given a glimpse into the life of Jesus Christ, our Lord and Savior," he said. "At Christmas we consider the love God showed by sending His Son to the earth.

"Easter is grace. And except for God's grace we'd all live in a dark world, lacking the love we've been given so generously. If you don't know Him already, Jesus Christ can be the greatest love of your life. Just as young Chase demonstrated on the cross tonight, Jesus stretched out His arms to show us exactly how much He loved us.

"His gift is nothing we can buy or earn with good deeds. It's freely given with great love, and all He asks in return is that we love and serve Him. He's a refuge when the burdens of the world become too heavy. Our friend and constant companion.

"The altar is open to anyone who feels the need to come forth and give his or her life to Jesus. If you don't know what to pray, members of our congregation are here to pray with you.

"It's a difficult walk, but it gets easier with that first step. With every head bowed and every eye closed, let's sing 'Amazing Grace.' If you don't know the words, just listen and be rewarded by this wonderful song."

Kim was the first person to kneel at the altar. She thanked God for His forgiveness and offered Him praise for the success of their efforts. Others soon joined her, and she knew joy untold when Wyatt knelt at her side. Chase came down from the stage and knelt by his father.

"Hey, Dad, can I lead you in the sinner's prayer?"

Wyatt hugged his son close and whispered, "I'd be honored."

Kim looked up, and Pastor Joe motioned her over and whispered, "Kneel and pray with anyone needing assistance." He motioned for Mari, Natalie, and other adults from the play to do the same.

Members of the choir stood in the audience and continued to sing as more church members stepped forward to pray with the unsaved surrounding the altar.

After at least a dozen people accepted Jesus Christ as their Savior, Pastor Joe held up his hand to stop the music.

"You're all invited to join the cast for refreshments in the church fellowship hall. Just follow the hallway. Now I think we should give the cast and volunteers another round of applause."

After the applause died down, he said, "The church will remain open for any of you who would like to return and pray at the altar."

A jubilant group gathered in the fellowship hall.

The dessert table held the donations from Avery, Natalie, and other members of the congregation. As usual, Natalie had outdone herself, and several smaller cakes with photos from the play airbrushed on them sat on the table. She stood nearby with a knife in hand.

"They're too pretty to eat!" Kim cried when she started to serve.

"Don't worry. I took photos for you. Plus I have the photos I used on the cakes themselves. They're from the rehearsal."

Kim felt someone's hand on her shoulder and turned to find Beth standing there. "Wasn't Chase wonderful?"

The woman's eyes were bright with unshed tears. "He was perfect for the role. And then when Wyatt. . .I'm so happy."

Kim hugged her and whispered, "I thought I'd lose it when Chase came down in that white robe and knelt to pray with his father."

"I know," Beth said softly.

Kim glanced around the room. "Where are your parents?"

"Over there with Wyatt. I just wanted to tell you how much we enjoyed the play."

"Thanks for all your help."

Beth squeezed her hand and stepped aside for the next person to offer their congratulations. Kim made the rounds, speaking to the parents, saying how much she enjoyed their children, and inviting those who didn't attend the church to visit Cornerstone again.

She grabbed a plate of food and took a minute to rest her feet when Wyatt came over to sit with her.

"Too bad the local paper doesn't do reviews," he commented. "The public would demand an encore performance."

Kim smiled at him. "The children did a wonderful job. Makes all my doubts seem so insignificant."

"I know it certainly affected me."

"I'm so happy for you, Wyatt. I know Chase is ecstatic."

"I feel good," he admitted. "It's something I should have done years ago when I convinced myself I didn't need a relationship with God. Now I know I do."

"We all do," Kim said. "We were created to worship. We may spend years searching, but God is all we need."

He nodded. "I'm looking forward to the future."

"Thanks for coming, Wyatt. The play wouldn't have been the same without your efforts."

"God has been at work in a number of lives lately. I'm thankful mine is one of them."

He hugged her and said good night.

❧

Early Easter Sunday, Kim was seated in the sanctuary for the sunrise service when Wyatt and Chase entered. Her parents, whose seats she was saving, were talking with friends a few pews back.

"Mind if we sit with you?"

She slid over to make room for them. "Not at all."

"You look beautiful. I like your Easter suit."

"I like yours, too."

"What, this old thing?" he asked, pulling on the lapels of the suit he wore.

Kim laughed. "Chase has already told me you two went shopping for new suits yesterday."

Wyatt grinned at his son. "You can dress him up, but you can't take him anywhere."

"You both look very handsome."

"Pastor Joe will be preaching to a full house today," Wyatt said, glancing around at the pews.

"Wonderful play, Kim." She smiled at the member who complimented her. Her fear that change would hurt the church proved itself unjustified as several more people gave their compliments before the pianist played the opening music. Her heart filled to overflowing when some of the older members took time to tell Wyatt how glad they were to see him at Cornerstone again.

When her parents returned to their seats, they greeted Wyatt and Chase. At her mother's questioning look, Kim shook her head and turned her attention to the pulpit.

As always, the message of Easter brought tears to her eyes.

"As some of you are aware, we started a beautification fund a while back." Pastor Joe walked over and untied the string that held the curtain in place. "Today we dedicate the Good Shepherd window. May it represent the grace and love of Jesus Christ to all those who enter Cornerstone Community Church."

The fabric fluttered to the floor, exposing the Good Shepherd and His sheep in the stained-glass window.

"It's beautiful," Kim whispered in awe.

"Isn't it, though?" Wyatt agreed.

After the service Pastor Joe gave an altar call, inviting anyone who cared to join the church to come forward. Wyatt moved to the front of the church and spoke to the minister before taking a front row seat.

Afterward Pastor Joe invited the congregation to extend the right hand of fellowship to the new members.

Kim smiled as she shook his hand. "Welcome to Cornerstone, Wyatt."

"Thanks, Kim."

"Your salvation means a great deal to a number of people. I

hate to welcome and run, but I need to get home and work on lunch. Maggie's joining us."

"We're going to Mom and Dad's." He squeezed her hand. "Thanks again, Kim."

"Happy Easter, Wyatt."

fifteen

"So what do you think about Wyatt Alexander joining Cornerstone?" her mother asked as they worked together in the kitchen.

"I'm very happy for him and his family."

"Do you love him?"

"He's a friend."

Her mother appeared skeptical. "If you say so, but I suspect you're in deeper than you realize."

Kim lifted the pot lid and checked the green beans. Giving them a final stir, she poured them into a bowl. "I have no doubt Jesus can make a difference in Wyatt, but he has a long path ahead of him. I'm holding firm to my vow."

"I suspect you'll have your hands full, making him understand you're interested in him only as a friend."

"I gave God control of my love life, Mom. I have to await His answer."

The doorbell rang, and her mother squeezed Kim's hand in understanding before going to answer the door. Kim could hear her welcoming Maggie. They came into the kitchen and, after catching up, talked about the Elliotts' journeys in their RV.

"The places you've visited sound wonderful." Maggie looked at Kim. "We should leave them here to handle things and go see for ourselves."

Her mom laughed. "As long as Jimmy could play golf, he wouldn't complain."

Maggie sighed. "Maybe one day I can get away. But I have to go back to work next week."

Kim's mother slid her arm about Maggie's waist. "That was a wonderful thing you did for Mrs. Allene."

"I loved her a great deal."

She nodded. "Kim told me about the house. Have you worked through that yet?"

"Not really. We went to the lawyer's office the other day, and I offered to sign it back over to Dillon. The lawyer objected, though. He said Mrs. Allene said I'd do that, and she wanted me to have the house. Now I feel like I'm dishonoring her wishes by saying no."

"I agree. Allene knew what she wanted. You've been like a daughter to her these past few years."

"I never expected anything more than her friendship. She also listed several items from her house that she wanted me to have."

"Well, Dillon will have to come to grips with his mother's will. Although he inherited his mother's house, I doubt he plans to stick around. He hasn't lived here for years."

"Maybe he's considering an investment for his retirement years," Kim suggested as she pulled the ham from the oven.

"Mrs. Allene told me he's fairly well-to-do," Maggie said.

"So he doesn't even need the rental house," Kim said. "He probably sees his mother's actions as a slight to his being her only child. I can't believe he's still treating you this way," she added.

Maggie looked at Kim's mother. "Let's drop the subject before we get Kim stirred up."

"Doesn't take much for that," her mother said.

"Hey, no dissing the cook allowed."

They laughed. "What can we do to help?"

"Everything's ready."

Kim arranged the items along the island front, using it as a buffet. Her mom called her dad to the table.

"Maggie," Kim's dad said as he walked into the kitchen,

opening his arms. "Good to see you."

"You, too, Mr. Jimmy. Retirement agrees with you."

"I can't complain. We've seen a lot of the states in our travels."

"And a lot of golf courses, I hear," Maggie teased.

"My fair share," he countered with a grin.

Everyone enjoyed the meal and reminisced about past Easters. "Did Cornerstone have its egg hunt this year?" her mother asked.

Kim nodded. "Mari said they had a good turnout."

"This has been a memorable Easter. Seeing our daughter's play performed so beautifully was such a blessing."

"Kimmie did good," her dad said.

"I can't take the credit. The play was nothing without the children and the adults who gave their all."

Her father lifted his tea glass. "Here's to Cornerstone's success."

"Here, here," Maggie said, tapping her glass against his.

"So when does your kitchen renovation start?" her mother asked.

"We talked about this month, but it depends on where Wyatt stands with the cabinets. He took measurements a few weeks ago. You won't know the place when we finish."

"Do you have the plans here?" her mother asked.

"Wyatt has my folder. I'm getting everything I've always wanted."

"Good thing it's a small kitchen," her dad said.

"I started a kitchen fund when I bought the condo."

"I'm eager to see the end result," Maggie said.

After lunch they cleared the table and moved to the living room. The afternoon passed quickly, and soon Maggie said good-bye so Kim could have some time alone with her parents. They were leaving again on Wednesday.

"It was wonderful seeing you both," Maggie declared, giving them each a hug. "Have fun in Florida."

"There's room if you want to tag along," Kim's dad offered.

"Hey, you didn't invite me along!" Kim exclaimed.

"Someone has to keep the business running," her father said.

"He only invited me because he knows I play golf," Maggie teased.

sixteen

Kim found she missed the practices and deadlines and knew life would have been boring without the kitchen renovation. On Thursday Wyatt called to tell her to pack up the kitchen. He arrived with help on Saturday morning, and they gutted the room in a few hours, leaving nothing more than an empty shell.

"We're going to pick up the cabinets and start putting them in place. Did you order the appliances?"

Kim nodded. "They have them in stock. I need to call when we're ready for them."

"Good idea. I think maybe by next Monday. Did you decide on flooring yet?"

"I'm still waffling between hardwood and tile."

"The wood might be better since you're having granite countertops. Have you considered expanding it into the living room?"

"I'm thinking about it."

"You need to decide soon." He hesitated. "What are you doing next Saturday? I promised Chase an outing to the beach. Want to come with us?"

Kim thought about the invitation. Spring fever had struck, and she was ready to enjoy the sunshine, but she wasn't sure. "You and Chase would have more fun alone," she said instead.

"I can't swim with him."

Kim had forgotten about Wyatt's missing foot. "Sure. Okay. You can come here, and we can go down to the beach from here."

"Beth suggested that, too. She said we could come up to her condo to shower and change."

"Sounds like a plan. If you finish my kitchen, I'll fix us something to eat."

"Are you trying to tempt me to work faster?"

"Of course not," Kim said with a broad grin.

"Good. It won't work. Your kitchen is a work in progress. Besides, everybody knows we need junk food to make the day worthwhile."

"What time?"

"Is nine too early?"

"We'd probably need to go a bit later. The water will be cold without the sun."

Wyatt shrugged. "I haven't walked in the water for a long time."

"Wear shorts, and we'll give it a test run."

"I don't want people staring at my prosthesis."

"Everything gets easier with practice, Wyatt. After a couple of looks most people accept things and move on."

"Can you?" he asked.

"I don't know why not. Does Chase have a problem?"

"He's intrigued. I had to show him how the prosthesis worked when he came to stay with me. He seems okay with it now."

"So maybe I'll be intrigued, too," Kim said in an effort to lighten the discussion. "You'll have to show me how it works."

"I can do that."

❧

The Saturday of their outing dawned clear and bright. The weather report promised no rain, and Kim hoped it was right. She hated those surprise rains that left a person damp and out of sorts.

All week she'd told herself she was doing this only to help a friend. But she'd taken time to buy new clothes that included a one-piece swimsuit, a pair of capri pants, and a print shirt. She'd even bought a new pair of sneakers.

Wyatt had made progress in the kitchen. All the new cabinets were in place, and the countertop was scheduled for Monday. The hardwood floor and tile installations had been completed on Friday.

Of course, all sorts of details still needed to be handled, including plumbing and lighting. And she needed to finalize her paint choice.

When the doorbell rang, Kim quickly wrapped her sarong about her waist and slipped on her flip-flops. She grabbed her beach blanket and tote bag on the way out. "Ready?"

Chase wore his swim trunks with a T-shirt, and Wyatt had on khaki shorts with a T-shirt and sandals. Kim caught herself glancing down at his artificial limb. "You'll do."

He seemed uncomfortable. "We'll see."

"Let's find a place on the beach before it fills up."

They rode the elevator and took the stairs down to the beach. Already people dotted the area. "How about here?" Kim asked, spreading the beach blanket. Chase and Wyatt nodded agreement.

"Ready to get wet, Chase?"

"Yeah," he responded enthusiastically.

"Hold on," she said, pulling a tube of sunscreen from her bag. "Put some of this on."

Kim had already applied her sunscreen, so she untied the sarong, kicked off her flip-flops, and said, "Race you to the water."

The two of them played in the waves for several minutes before Kim suggested they head back to the beach. Chase shook his hair, spraying water all over his dad. Wyatt grabbed his son and wrestled him to the blanket.

Kim grabbed a towel from her tote. "Here, Chase, dry your hair." He dried off a little, then started down the beach to study a jellyfish that had washed up on shore. She noticed Wyatt staring at her. "What?"

"I've never seen you without makeup. You look good."

"The beach is the only place I go without my war paint."

"You don't need it. You have beautiful eyes."

Kim could feel her cheeks grow warm. "Thanks. Did you hear from Beth yet?"

Wyatt nodded. "The move is definite. They've been assigned military housing."

"How is Chase adapting?" She spotted him wandering in the distance.

"I think he's okay. He's picked out paint for his room and wants me to build a bookcase and desk."

"Is he planning to help?"

"Do you doubt it?"

Chase had shown more than a passing interest in the work being done in her kitchen when he'd accompanied his father.

"He's been looking for plans online. He's even found the complicated plans to build secret compartments."

"Every kid needs a hiding place."

"He's got Ole Blue sleeping on a rug by his bed. I told him Blue was a yard dog, but he broke me down."

Kim laughed. "I bet that dog is in heaven with a kid in the picture."

"They get along well."

"Let's explore with him a bit," Kim suggested.

"You go ahead. I'll wait here."

Kim shook her head. "It's your day with your son. You can't sit on the beach and leave him to entertain himself. Nor can you expect me to entertain him."

"Okay," Wyatt growled, removing his sandals. "This will probably be a first for this beach. Prepare yourself for the finger pointing and whispering."

"I'll ignore them if you will."

"Deal." They shook on it, and Wyatt retained his grasp of Kim's hand.

The two of them walked along the shore to where Chase danced in a shallow pool of water. "Hey, Dad!" he called. "Did you see that monster jellyfish back there?"

"Sure did. Be careful around them. They have quite a sting."

"You ever get stung?"

"I stepped on one in the water once."

"Hey, if you stepped on him with your fake foot, he couldn't hurt you," Chase said.

Kim looked at Wyatt and smiled. "That's one way of looking at it. You guys want to build a sandcastle? I have some buckets in my condo storage unit."

"Let's build something different," Wyatt suggested.

"Can we make a gator or a croc?" Chase asked eagerly. "I like gators best."

"You wouldn't if one of them got you in his teeth." Kim grabbed him about the waist.

"Oh, he's too tough to be good gator bait," Wyatt teased, ruffling his son's hair.

Chase grinned at his dad. "You're tougher than me."

The three of them were still on the beach at around one o'clock. Chase and Wyatt showed amazing talent with their sand crocodile and drew several interested onlookers.

Kim stood up and brushed the sand off her hands. "You guys ready for a shower and a snack?"

"Dad said we could get hot dogs."

"Well, let's get moving then. I'm ready for lunch."

Back at the condos they went their separate ways to shower and change. Wyatt exchanged his shorts for khaki slacks, but Kim didn't push the issue. A trip to the beach was a major accomplishment.

Wyatt and Chase took her to a little hot dog place they'd found and liked.

"Hope you like this place," Wyatt said as he held the door for Kim.

"I love a good hot dog."

After they received their food and slipped into a booth, they prayed, then attacked their food with the healthy appetite of people who had spent hours in the sun.

"Dad, can we play putt-putt this afternoon?"

"What do you think, Kim?"

She laughed. "My dad would love him."

They chose the largest place on King's Highway and spent the next couple of hours challenging each other. Afterward, they climbed into the truck and went to the arcade. There they crowded into a photo booth and made faces at the camera. Kim couldn't keep up with the men as they ate cotton candy, snow cones, and ice cream and downed mega cups of soda.

"You guys ready to call it a day?" Kim asked. "I need to check in at the store."

"Ah, do we have to?"

Wyatt placed his hand on his son's shoulder. "You heard Miss Kim. She has things to do. And I promised Aunt Beth we'd take your grandmother to the grocery store."

"I forgot."

"We'll do this again," Wyatt promised.

They walked back to the truck, and Wyatt drove Kim home.

Kim said, "You guys sure you don't want to finish my kitchen tonight?"

"Can we, Dad?"

"I'm teasing, Chase. We can't do anything else until we get the countertops in."

"What will you do for dinner?" the boy asked.

"My fridge is in the living room with my microwave. I have some food I can heat and eat."

"Can we remodel our kitchen, Dad?"

"Not now. We need to build your desk and bookcases."

"Can we work on those tonight?"

"I don't think so. After we visit your grandparents, we need to study our Sunday school lessons." He glanced at Kim. "Did I tell you I signed up for the new Christians' class?"

"Don't they do those on Sunday mornings during Sunday school?"

Wyatt nodded. "I want to join the Bible study class, too."

Kim recalled that first fire in a new Christian. "That's a good idea."

He parked in his sister's parking space. "Wait here, Chase. I'm going to walk Miss Kim upstairs and get those wet clothes we left in Beth's condo."

They took the elevator up to the second floor.

"I really enjoyed myself today."

Wyatt propped himself against the side of the elevator. "I did, too. And there's no telling when Chase will run down. I have a feeling we're going to work on the birdhouse tonight."

She laughed, and Wyatt did, too. Kim found the sound pleasing. "He doesn't want the day to end."

"Neither do I," Wyatt admitted. "Thanks for making it special."

"I didn't do anything but have fun."

"I need someone to teach me how to do that."

The elevator door opened, and she stepped into the walkway. "Follow Chase's lead. He'll keep you young."

Wyatt stepped out, too. "No, seriously, I need you in my life, Kim." She turned and looked up at him. "I'm not saying this very well, but I care a great deal for you."

"I care for you, too, Wyatt. You and Chase."

"As friends? Or could it be more?"

Could it be more? Kim already knew the answer in her

heart. Her feelings for Wyatt Alexander were strong, but she was afraid. Despite the feeling she should step out on faith, she couldn't help but wonder if she would be making a mistake.

"Only God knows what the future holds," she told him.

seventeen

Wyatt was in Kim's apartment when she arrived home Monday afternoon. She could see Chase doing his homework on the balcony.

"Whew." The scent of the stain filled her nostrils. "I'm surprised you have any sinuses left."

He grinned. "I took off the mask when I helped Chase get set up out there. I figured it's too smelly in here for him."

The balcony doors were open, and the ocean breezes helped a little.

"Did you fix him a snack?" Kim asked as she glanced through the mail.

"I picked him up from school, and we stopped on the way over here."

She moved closer to where he had touched up the stain on her new cabinets. "Oh, my counters," she cried, running her hand over the shiny black granite. "They're beautiful. I can't wait to see everything in place."

"The appliances arrive tomorrow. Did you set up a plumber to connect the icemaker, dishwasher, and sink?"

Kim nodded. "He's coming on Thursday."

"So you'll have a kitchen by the weekend. We should celebrate."

"I'll celebrate by putting my house back together."

"You can do that anytime. I'm offering a picnic at Brookgreen Gardens. Just the two of us. Chase is spending the day with Beth." He appeared excited by the idea.

"I do work, you know."

"Can't you get someone to cover for you?" he asked with a

hint of disappointment in his tone.

"Why Brookgreen Gardens?"

Wyatt shrugged. "I thought about what you might enjoy. I considered the theaters but don't know what you've seen or want to see. Then I thought about the gardens and figured the fresh air and statuary would appeal to you."

"I haven't been to the gardens since I was a kid," she admitted.

"Say yes, Kim."

"The best I can offer is I'll let you know."

"Oh, come on. You know you want to."

Kim shook her head at his coaxing. "I think you're jumping the gun. My kitchen isn't completed." Her nose wrinkled as the fumes filled her head. "How much of that stuff are you planning to put on today?"

"Just this coat. Beth said you could sleep over at her place if it's too strong. She's coming back to pack. That's one reason she wants Chase. He has to sort through his stuff and decide what's going to my house."

"So you've agreed to make it a permanent thing?"

"We're going to see what Chase thinks Friday night."

"I'm sure he'll want to stay with you."

Wyatt looked hopeful. "I've enjoyed having him around. I've missed out on so much of his life."

Kim prayed Chase would choose his father. She knew losing his son at this point would break Wyatt's heart. "I have a good feeling about you two," Kim said. "Decide what you want me to do while I change."

As she traded her work clothes for an old pair of jeans and a T-shirt, Kim thought about how much she'd enjoyed having Wyatt around lately. Coming home to him and Chase most afternoons had brightened her former quiet existence.

With her parents on the road she missed having family nearby. Maggie had returned to work, and Mari was busy with her family. Julie and Noah were doing the newlywed thing, and Natalie was busy as well.

Maybe she would agree to go with him. She hadn't seen Brookgreen Gardens in years. And secretly Kim admitted it pleased her that Wyatt had thought about what she might enjoy.

Back in the kitchen Kim helped stain the island cabinets. They talked about a variety of topics, including the Bible study class Wyatt attended. The group was studying the book of Romans, and Kim had been reading along to keep up with his questions.

"You promise to think about Saturday?" he asked.

"Okay, I'll agree to the gardens if you let me provide the picnic."

"Sounds like a plan. Chase and I have enjoyed those dinners you and Maggie prepared."

28

As they entered the gardens on Saturday, Kim admired the fighting stallion sculpture that welcomed them.

"Beautiful work," she commented.

Wyatt was in a good mood. Chase had chosen to live with his dad even though he wanted to visit his aunt regularly as well. Wyatt had no problem with that. It was the least he could do after all he'd put them through. He paid their admission and followed the signs to the picnic area where they spread the food on the table.

Wyatt said, "I think you must be blessed when it comes to good weather and outings. Last time we came we brought my grandmother, my aunt, and my cousins. It started to rain the minute they laid out the food, so we had to grab everything and jump back into the car to wait it out.

"Then things went from bad to worse. My grandmother could get around, but she was slow. Every time she was a hundred feet away from the car, the rain started. We spent the day walking around with umbrellas. We found a wheelchair for Granny, and two of my cousins pushed her so fast she nearly ended up in the reflecting pool. The adults took control of the chair after that. My dad stopped at one point and said he was never coming back to the gardens."

Kim struggled to keep from laughing. "Did he?"

"No."

They laughed together. "We had the same kind of outings," Kim said. "There's nothing like cowering under a shelter with a hundred other people while the storm rages on."

"I have something for you."

Kim opened the wrapped package to find a beautifully carved cross box. "I thought the cross might remind you of our first meeting. Then again, maybe it would be best if I didn't remind you of that."

"It's beautiful. And I'll always remember how you helped me with the play. Thank you so much."

"Open it."

Kim lifted the lid to find an exquisite cut-diamond ring tucked into the folds of velvet he'd placed inside the box.

Startled, she looked at him. "I don't understand."

"I love you, Kim."

"Wyatt?"

"Wait. Hear me out. I know I've blindsided you with this, but I wanted to state my intentions. I enjoy being with you. After Karen I never believed I'd love again, but you changed that. I know we can have a good life."

"How can you be sure?" she asked. "When it comes to love, I've made more mistakes than I care to count. Truthfully I'm not sure I'm capable of making any relationship work. I wouldn't want to hurt you or Chase."

"You wouldn't," Wyatt said, shaking his head.

"There's so much I have to let go of before I could be a good wife. I have serious trust issues when it comes to men."

"You can trust me," Wyatt told her. "After we married, Karen was the only woman in my life. I didn't cheat on her or lie to her. I worked hard to provide for her and my son."

"But your life fell apart."

"Because we didn't have God. Don't get me wrong," he said when she started to object. "I know there's no promise life will be perfect with God in it, but I believe it's better because He's there for us. I have many regrets. My stupidity cost me a great deal, but I'm ready to move on. To have you as my wife, to give Chase a couple of siblings, and to make my house a home again."

"Oh, Wyatt, I can't say yes."

"That's okay, Kim. I didn't expect you to agree right away."

She felt confused. "Then why did you buy a ring?"

"To show I'm not giving up. I intend to persevere just as God has persevered all these years to make me His. I've prayed about this. I know we're right for each other, and I think that once you give your doubts over to God you'll agree."

She pushed the box back across the table toward him.

Wyatt rested his hand on top of hers. "Keep it. If you decide you can't marry me, you can return the ring, but the box is yours—a symbol of how God used you to touch my heart."

His words caused her to tear up. "I'm so sorry, Wyatt. Please don't think I don't love you and Chase. I just have to be sure. I can't risk having my heart broken again."

Wyatt looked almost sad. "You know, Kim, I think you should look at Chase as a prime example of how God works through us. My son has absolutely no reason to love me. I was a vague, shadowy figure in the background of his life, but when I came out of the darkness he welcomed me with open arms. He prayed for my salvation and loves me with the innocence of a child. Who does that remind you of?"

"Jesus," she whispered.

Wyatt nodded. "I can't begin to promise to have Chase's ability to love so easily, but one thing is for sure—without God's grace I'd be more lost than I've ever been. Today and for the rest of my life I have a promise of light. I'd like for you to share that light with me."

When she didn't say anything, Wyatt only said, "Eat up. We have lots to see."

eighteen

"What did you do yesterday?" Maggie asked at the fellowship following church the next morning. "I called the store to see if you wanted to go to dinner, but Ruby said you were off."

"I spent the day at Brookgreen Gardens with Wyatt," she admitted.

"I've never been there. I've heard the area is beautiful."

Kim was surprised Maggie didn't comment on her date with Wyatt. "I enjoyed myself. The statuary is outstanding, and they have so many other activities."

"I'm sure spending time with Wyatt made it even more fun."

"Oh, Maggie, I'm so confused," Kim told her. "I know Wyatt has given his life to God, but I can't get past the feeling that no one changes overnight."

"Do you feel God expects that of us?"

Kim shrugged. "I don't want to give away another chunk of my heart to a man who isn't interested in being there for me."

"And you think Wyatt would do that?"

"I'm too afraid of being hurt to take the risk."

"People in happy, loving relationships get hurt, too, Kim. But they communicate, forgive, forget, and move on with their lives. Have you put your life on pause forever because of the last guy you dated?"

Kim grimaced at the thought. "I guess I have."

"And you want to stay there, locked in the misery you feel?"

"No, I want a husband and children."

"Then shouldn't you be listening to God instead of yourself? How can God send you someone to love if you doubt every man He sends?"

Kim tossed the empty coffee cup into the trash. "How do I determine the ones He sends? Wyatt has a considerable past to deal with. I'm afraid his baggage and my own would be too much for us as a couple."

"Has he indicated it's more than a friendship?"

"He proposed."

Maggie gasped and grabbed Kim's hand, pulling her over to a private corner. "And you didn't call me?"

"I was in shock," Kim admitted. "Before the picnic, he handed me a hand-carved cross box. It's beautiful."

Maggie nodded. "Get to the part about the proposal. Did he give you a ring?"

"Yes, he put it in the box. The ring is beautiful. Expensive."

"What did you say?"

"That I wasn't ready yet. He's willing to wait."

"Did you have any idea?"

"He's made references to the future and needing me in his life. How can I be sure it's not seeing him so often with the kitchen renovation? Now that that's done, maybe I can get my jumbled life back in order—and be able to think more clearly."

"Good luck," Maggie said with more than a little sarcasm. "When you figure it out, let me know how. I haven't sorted out my thoughts since Mrs. Allene's death."

"I've seen Dillon here at Cornerstone a few times. Mrs. Allene would be pleased to know he's attending regularly—though I thought he'd be gone by now."

"He's decided to stay for the summer."

"Any word on the house?"

"He told me to call off my defenders. Said he got the message. What does that mean?" Maggie asked, her expression perplexed.

"You don't think someone confronted him about his behavior, do you?"

"Surely not," Maggie whispered. "I'd never want anyone to do that."

It occurred to Kim that Maggie and Dillon would make a nice couple. She must have love on the brain. "I think we have some powerful praying to do," Kim said. "I should tell Mari, Natalie, and Julie."

"Since you have the renovated kitchen to show off, why don't we plan a lunch at your place next week?"

Kim grinned. "Or we could go out and I could talk about my new kitchen."

"You don't have to cook. We can all bring something."

"I'll take care of everything," Kim promised. "And I'll be in prayer for you. You do the same for me."

⁂

It was the following Thursday night before the women could arrange their schedules to get together for dinner. Mari, Julie, and Maggie arrived together.

"Where's Natalie?" Kim asked.

"She has to drop off a birthday cake, and then she'll be here," Julie said. "She's bringing a special treat."

"Umm. Natalie's treats are always worthwhile."

"I think she's using us as taste testers," Julie told them. "She's experimenting with some new chocolate ideas and wants our opinion. She's getting ready to branch out into something new."

"I hope she doesn't overdo," Maggie said.

"I think she'll be sensible," Mari told them. "Look what she gave up when she realized it was too stressful for her. Hey, let's see this wonderful new kitchen."

The women oohed and aahed over the renovated kitchen. "Maybe one day I'll get my own cabinetry by Alexander," Maggie said, running her hand along the smooth finish. "This is gorgeous."

"I wouldn't mind some new cabinets myself," Mari said.

"Think the church would spring for a kitchen renovation?"

"I could donate—," Julie began.

"Don't even think about it," Mari interrupted.

"She's as bad as Joey," Julie grumbled. "They won't let me do anything."

Mari wrapped her arm about Julie's shoulder. "You help in more tangible ways. It's nice having an instant babysitter." She turned to Kim. "So what's for dinner?"

"Have a seat in the living room. I have appetizers."

Kim carried in a tray of veggies, fruits, and dips and poured water with lemon for everyone. "I kept it light."

"I'm delighted with any meal I don't have to prepare," Julie said.

"Did you and Noah find a place yet?" Kim asked after handing Julie a glass.

"Not yet. Noah thought Beth Erikson might want to sell her place, but she's planning to rent it week to week."

"I think she wants to keep it so she can vacation here."

"Cheaper than shelling out a couple of thousand for a week at the beach," Julie agreed.

The doorbell rang, and Kim excused herself.

"Sorry I'm late, but these will make up for it." Natalie slid the tray onto the new countertop, looking around. "You really did this place up right."

"Thanks," Kim said, checking out the chocolate-covered fruit and candies. "You didn't have to bring anything, but we're glad you did. What would you like to drink?"

"You have any soda? I've been craving it for weeks, but I don't dare keep any in the house."

"Caffeine-free okay?"

"Sounds wonderful."

The women visited for a few minutes longer before they moved to the table for the meal. Everyone enjoyed the lemon chicken and rice pilaf with green beans.

"That kitchen must have some powerful effects on your cooking abilities," Maggie teased. "I didn't know you had it in you."

"I can cook, I just hate cooking for one."

"I know what you mean," Natalie agreed. "Good thing I like salads."

"Kim, when are you going to tell them?" Maggie asked.

"Tell us what?" Julie asked eagerly.

"Wyatt proposed," Maggie volunteered.

"Do you mind?" Kim said with a look of dismay.

The other three women glanced from one to the other. "Okay, give," Julie demanded.

"Wyatt and I went out last Saturday, and he gave me this." She slid the box on the table.

"Oh, that's beautiful!" Mari cried, running her finger along the carving.

Kim nodded. "He said it's to remind me of our first meeting."

"So how did he propose?" Natalie asked.

"Lift the lid."

One by one the women studied the diamond inside.

"I was speechless."

"You told him no, didn't you?" Julie guessed.

Kim glanced down at the box that rested in her hands. "Actually, I told him I wasn't sure."

"Why?" Natalie asked.

"I have to be sure."

"You think he doesn't love you?" Julie asked.

"No. I'm sure about that. I just don't know if either of us can get beyond our pasts and move on."

"Don't let the past keep you from being happy. I nearly lost Noah for that very reason," Julie told her. "I judged him wrongly, and what we have today would never have happened if God hadn't directed our paths. I've never been happier, and I owe it all to God."

"I love Wyatt and Chase, but the fear of risking my heart again scares me to death."

"My very wise husband once reminded me God didn't give me the sense of fear," Julie said.

"What do you want most in the world, Kim?" Mari asked.

"To be loved and have a family."

"Then you know what you have to do, don't you?"

"Pray harder?" Kim asked with a playful grimace.

"We'll pray with you," Maggie said. "I like Wyatt. Of course, if you married him you'd have to give up this wonderful kitchen."

"Who says?" Kim asked. "He could live here."

"But it would be more feasible for you to live at his house. His business is there."

"We have a ways to go before we reach that point."

"You think?" Julie teased. "I'd say you're closer to saying yes than you realize."

More than a little afraid Julie might be right, Kim changed the subject. "And what about Natalie? Aren't we concerned she's taking on too much?"

Natalie snorted. "You have to be talking about work. Everyone knows the only man I have chasing after me wants to run me out of town."

"No change between you and Avery?" Mari asked.

Natalie shook her head. "Now he's angry because I offered to help with the props. And because my photo cakes were noticed at the play reception. And maybe because it rained last Tuesday. Who knows?"

"Another reason we need to be in prayer for each other," Kim said.

"I already pray for each of you every day," Mari said.

They all nodded.

"Let's pray more specific prayers," Julie suggested. "That Kim can work out her relationship with Wyatt, Maggie and

Dillon can come to an agreement over the estate, Maggie and Natalie will find the loves of their lives—and that I learn to keep my mouth shut."

"What about me?" Mari asked.

"We just thank God for you."

"Amen to that. Natalie, pull that tray of chocolates over here and tell us what you're planning," Kim said.

Dessert turned into the best part of the meal.

"I'm thinking of offering chocolate parties. I bought a chocolate fountain, and it got me to thinking it would be a good party-catering activity."

"Would you try to do it alone?"

"You don't have to worry about me. I know my limitations. I remember that attack, and I don't ever plan to have another one."

Mari held out her hand, and Julie grasped it in hers. They continued until they formed a circle around the table.

"Let's seek God's guidance."

nineteen

The power of prayer kept Kim going over the next few days. Now that Wyatt had finished the kitchen she didn't see him daily, but they talked on the phone every night just before bed. He'd promised not to rush her, and he hadn't.

They discussed their families and work, and Wyatt shared scriptures he'd read. She thought about how wonderful it would be to have him there with her. The first time he spoke of how different the church was from what he remembered, Kim whispered a prayer of thanks. She suspected God was working His changes in Wyatt.

He sat with her during church services, and she'd joined the Bible study. She helped him stain when he had a deadline, and he'd done a couple of favors for her at Eclectics. She'd even helped build Chase's bookcase and desk, figuring out how to make the secret drawers for the desk.

She joined his family for Sunday lunch a couple of times. The experience gave Kim a glimpse into Wyatt's relationship with his father. The man had high expectations for his son and grandson and didn't mind voicing his opinion. Knowing Wyatt had made his peace with his father had done her heart a world of good.

Chase was playing soccer, and he invited her to his games. Kim enjoyed sitting in the bleachers with Wyatt and cheering for his son.

Everything was fine until she allowed fear to take control. Wyatt had become adept at figuring out the worst times for her, and those were the times when he backed off.

The past Saturday they'd gone out to breakfast, and while

dining alfresco they shared the paper. She was taken aback by an old boyfriend's wedding announcement and voiced her thoughts. "What does she have that I didn't?"

"I'm thankful," Wyatt said when she tossed down the paper. "God intended you for me."

"Maybe He doesn't intend me for anyone."

"He does," Wyatt returned. "Having you in my life has made a major change in me. I am the happiest I have ever been."

Kim smiled at the thought. "I am happy, too, until I give in to these pity parties."

He squeezed her hand. "Then don't. Let yourself love and be loved."

"I'm trying." A tiny smile touched her mouth. "There's another major issue standing in the way of my decision."

"What's that?" he asked curiously.

"I could never give up my kitchen."

Wyatt laughed hard. "But wouldn't you prefer a house to the condo?"

"I suppose if I settled some of the details in my mind I might not feel so overwhelmed. We should talk about what we both expect of marriage."

They drove to the beach and strolled along the sandy shore. Even at that early hour the beach was filled with families and sunbathers enjoying the beautiful spring weather. The roar of the waves provided a soothing background for their discussion.

"I could sell the house, and we could live in your condo," Wyatt offered.

"But your business. Ole Blue."

"I'd have to find another place to do my woodwork. And a home for the dog. But I'd do it for you."

"It wouldn't be fair to Chase. He's getting used to your place. You have to think about him, too."

"It's not as if he's not used to the condos."

"And you're willing to turn your life upside down to have me as your wife?"

"Not exactly," Wyatt said. "I'm willing to make sacrifices, but I'd expect equal consideration from you."

"We both know marriage is about give and take, Wyatt. But you'd be miserable in the condo, and you know it."

"We could sell both places and find something we all like."

Kim bent to pick up a seashell and examined the detail before dropping it onto the sand. "The condo isn't enough for a larger family."

"So you're agreeable to children?"

"Of course I am."

"That's one major issue out of the way. What about work? Do I need to find a job that pays better?"

"Would more money make you happier?"

"It's about supporting a wife and family, Kim."

"I have my income from Eclectics. I hadn't planned to stop working when I marry."

"So the only thing in question is where we'll live?"

"I think there's probably more to it than that."

Wyatt was silent for a few minutes longer before he stopped walking and reached for her hands. "Can I make a suggestion? I thought maybe we could talk to Pastor Joe about premarital counseling."

"But—"

Wyatt rested his finger against her lips. "It's a way to resolve more of your doubts."

"You don't have any doubts?"

"Not about making you my wife. My doubts have to do with my self-esteem. Mostly my handicap. And being a good husband and father."

"Do you think we might give people the wrong idea if we enrolled in premarital counseling?"

"What are you thinking, Kim? Is there any chance you'll marry me?"

"Wyatt. . .you know. . ."

"Sounds like we're both wasting our time," he said, releasing her hands. "I'll drop you at home and go pick up Chase."

Kim caught Wyatt's arm. "Talking to Pastor Joe is a good idea. Let's ask tomorrow after the service."

"Are you sure?"

"I care for you a great deal, and I'd never want to do anything to hurt you or Chase. If I didn't believe there was hope for us, I'd end this right now."

"Can you at least tell me what I'm fighting against? Are you expecting God to release you from your vow?"

"No. I'm more determined than ever to be sure I don't make another mistake."

"Does Chase frighten you?"

He raised a question she had considered. "What would I be to your son?"

"His mother, stepmother, guardian."

"But what do you expect of me?"

"To love and guide him in his life."

"And if we disagree? What if I see things differently from you?"

"I suspect you'd be softer on him than I'd be, Kim. I know what lies ahead for Chase. He's a good kid, and I pray he'll stay that way. But he's going to face some strong temptations. I don't want him to make the same mistakes I made. I know he may, but I pray he's willing to hear me out when the time comes. I have a lot to prove to both of you."

"A lot to prove." His words echoed in her mind. She had promised to seek God's guidance, and yet she had allowed fear to keep her from accepting the love of a good man. The man she now believed God had placed in her life. Relief flowed through Kim as she laid her hand on his arm. "Wyatt?"

He looked at her expectantly.

"The answer is yes."

Joy filled his blue eyes, with a wondrous smile covering his face. "To my proposal?"

"To everything. I'll marry you. I'll be the mother of your children. I'll live in your home. And I'll love you for the rest of my life."

Wyatt pulled her into his arms. "Oh, Kim, what changed your mind?"

"God answered my prayers. You don't need to prove anything to anyone, Wyatt. God accepts you just as you are, and so do I."

twenty

"It's a beautiful day for a wedding." Kim's mother placed the wreath of white baby roses about her daughter's head.

She watched her mother's reflection in the mirror as she stood behind her, pinning the shoulder-length veil into place. They had arrived two weeks before to help with the wedding and planned to stay until Kim and Wyatt returned from their honeymoon. "I was so happy to see the sun this morning," Kim said.

"Did Wyatt ever tell you where you're going on your honeymoon?"

"He finally told me last night that he's planned a long weekend in Charleston. Then we're coming home for Chase and taking a family vacation in Florida. We wanted to do something together before he goes back to school."

Kim turned to look at her mother. "You'll never guess what Wyatt gave me for a wedding present."

"Diamonds?"

"Better. He duplicated my kitchen at his place. You should have seen him and Chase. We went to the house after the rehearsal dinner. They were so excited they could hardly wait for me to open the door."

"That sounds more like a gift for the family than you."

"Oh, Mom, don't you see? The real gift is that he cares about what makes me happy."

"He's doing a good job."

"Wyatt tells me he loves me," Kim said with a big smile, "but he shows me in more ways than I can count."

After she'd said yes, they had decided to take their time and get to know each other better. Kim had enjoyed being Wyatt's fiancée. She'd never dreamed she'd find such a loving, caring man. Admittedly, at times, she expected to see the bad boy come through, but Wyatt worked hard at making sure that part of him was dead forever.

They had gone through premarital counseling, and only when they were both comfortable about getting married had they set the date. The last few months had been spent in a flurry of preparation.

Today, when she slipped into the white satin A-line dress with its sweetheart neckline, beaded bodice, and chapel train, Kim knew her every doubt had dissolved like snow in the summer heat.

She picked up a box from the countertop. "These are Wyatt's grandmother's diamond and pearl earrings."

"Something old and something borrowed," her mother said. "Here's your something new from your dad and me."

Kim opened the jewelry box and found inside a delicate gold necklace with a jeweled center. "Help me put it on."

"Do you have something blue?"

"My garter."

Her mother hugged her. "I'm happy for you, Kimmie."

"Ah, you're excited about becoming a grandmother," Kim said, giving her an extra squeeze.

"Not just me. You saw your dad and Chase fooling around last night during the rehearsal party. He's a great kid."

"We appreciate your helping Mrs. Alexander with Chase. Wyatt worries he's too much for his grandmother."

"It's been a few years since we did the parent-child thing, but I don't think we've forgotten how."

"How would you feel about a baby?" Kim asked. "Wyatt and I have talked about having a child right away."

Her mother's broad smile showed her approval. "Hold on to your condo. You give me a grandchild, and we're home to stay."

"Too late. I sold it to Noah and Julie Loughlin. Wyatt plans to put in connections for the RV at the house."

"You want us around for more than the occasional visit?" her mother asked with a teasing tone in her voice.

"You know I do," Kim told her, smiling. "There's always a place in my home for you and Daddy."

The door to the dressing area opened, and Mari, Maggie, Natalie, Beth, and Julie entered the room, wearing their tea-length, azalea-colored dresses.

"Okay, mother and daughter bonding time is over," Julie said. "You have an anxious groom and best boy out there."

Her dad tapped on the door. "Everyone ready? I have the photographer with me. He wants a shot of me with the bride."

Mari opened the door, and Kim's father came over to hug his daughter. "You're beautiful."

"Thanks, Daddy."

The photographer snapped several photos and left. There was a flurry of activity as Kim searched for her elbow-length white gloves. She pulled them on as her friends picked up their white rose bouquets, and Maggie passed Kim the red roses she'd chosen. Kim waited while her attendants moved slowly to the front of the church. When her turn came, her gaze fixed on Wyatt in his white tuxedo.

Kim had never been more thankful for waterproof mascara than when the joy of the moment overcame her. "Thank You, Lord," she whispered as they walked along the white runner that led her to Wyatt.

Her dad placed her hand in Wyatt's and stepped aside. Kim smiled at Wyatt, and he returned the smile. What a wonderful life she was going to have with him as her husband.

Time stood still from the moment Pastor Joe said, "Dearly beloved," until he pronounced them husband and wife and son.

"I love you," Wyatt said and kissed her to the applause of their family and friends.

As she turned to walk back down the aisle, the Good Shepherd window caught her attention. And Kim thanked Jesus for the grace that had brought her love.

A Letter To Our Readers

Dear Reader:

In order that we might better contribute to your reading enjoyment, we would appreciate your taking a few minutes to respond to the following questions. We welcome your comments and read each form and letter we receive. When completed, please return to the following:

Fiction Editor
Heartsong Presents
PO Box 719
Uhrichsville, Ohio 44683

1. Did you enjoy reading *Except for Grace* by Terry Fowler?
   ❑ Very much! I would like to see more books by this author!
   ❑ Moderately. I would have enjoyed it more if

   _____

   _____

   _____

2. Are you a member of **Heartsong Presents**? ❑ Yes ❑ No
   If no, where did you purchase this book? _____

   _____

3. How would you rate, on a scale from 1 (poor) to 5 (superior), the cover design? _____

4. On a scale from 1 (poor) to 10 (superior), please rate the following elements.

   _____ Heroine   _____ Plot
   _____ Hero   _____ Inspirational theme
   _____ Setting   _____ Secondary characters

5. These characters were special because? _____

_____

_____

6. How has this book inspired your life? _____

_____

_____

7. What settings would you like to see covered in future **Heartsong Presents** books? _____

_____

_____

8. What are some inspirational themes you would like to see treated in future books? _____

_____

_____

9. Would you be interested in reading other **Heartsong Presents** titles? ❏ Yes ❏ No

10. Please check your age range:
   ❏ Under 18   ❏ 18-24
   ❏ 25-34   ❏ 35-45
   ❏ 46-55   ❏ Over 55

Name _____

Occupation _____

Address _____

City, State, Zip_____

CAROLINA CARPENTER *Brides*

4 stories in 1

Four couples find tools for building romance in a home improvement store.

Janet Benrey, Ron Benrey, Lena Nelson Dooley, and Yvonne Lehman tell the tales of couples who find each other in the midst of daily life.

Contemporary, paperback, 352 pages, 5³⁄₁₆" x 8"

Heart♥ng

Any 12 Heartsong Presents titles for only $27.00*

CONTEMPORARY ROMANCE IS CHEAPER BY THE DOZEN!

Buy any assortment of twelve *Heartsong Presents* **titles and save 25% off the already discounted price of $2.97 each!**

*plus $3.00 shipping and handling per order and sales tax where applicable. If outside the U.S. please call 740-922-7280 for shipping charges.

HEARTSONG PRESENTS TITLES AVAILABLE NOW:

Presents

Great Inspirational Romance at a Great Price!

Heartsong Presents books are inspirational romances in
contemporary and historical settings, designed to give you an
enjoyable, spirit-lifting reading experience. You can choose
wonderfully written titles from some of today's best authors like
Andrea Boeshaar, Wanda E. Brunstetter, Yvonne Lehman, Joyce
Livingston, and many others.

When ordering quantities less than twelve, above titles are $2.97 each.
Not all titles may be available at time of order.

HP 7-07